CURSE OF THE ANCIENTS

1870's. A peaceful town in Iowa territory. The townspeople dislike their new visitor. An Indian man. But they are about to find out that the color of his skin is the least of their worries.

A young man, James Johnson, illegitimate son of the legendary Wyatt Earp, dreams of adventure and following in his daddy's footsteps. James and his mentally disabled friend, Carson, are about to come face to face with an evil previously unimaginable in their little town. An evil they invited in.

All hell's about to break loose.

Supernatural forces are at work and the body count is rising…

Curse of the Ancients is the first novel in the *Son of Earp* series by Chuck Buda.

ALSO BY CHUCK BUDA

Visit my website to find all these books, and more!
www.authorchuckbuda.com

CURSE OF THE ANCIENTS

CHUCK BUDA

CURSE OF THE ANCIENTS
Copyright © 2016 by Chuck Buda
Edited by Jenny Adams
ISBN: 978-1079105407
www.authorchuckbuda.com

Cover art © 2016 by Phil Yarnall | SMAYdesign.com
Interior design by Dullington Design Co.

The author greatly appreciates you taking the time to read his work. Please consider leaving a review wherever you bought this book or telling your friends or blog readers about this book to help spread the word.

Thank you for supporting my work. Without you the story would not be told.

Dedicated to my parents.
For always believing in me and putting up with all my "moments."

CURSE OF THE
ANCIENTS

CHAPTER 1

The sun blazed across the grassy plains like a bonfire. His dark skin glistened as he sprinted for the woods ahead. He leapt over a fallen tree in the knee-high golden grass. Afraid to glance behind, Crouching Bear lurched forward as he searched for places to hide and relief from the heat.

He knew his time was short. The tribe would be coming for him to avenge his mistake. The spirits might forgive him someday, but his people would not. They must make an example of him. It was how the tribe governed itself. Warriors were celebrated and men who failed to achieve this lofty status were demonized as less than men, or worse, cowards. Crouching Bear was no coward. And he wasn't a warrior either. At least, he wasn't any longer.

Crouching Bear studied the ways of the warrior soul. He spent countless months practicing among the elders, harnessing the great warrior spirit. He had proven himself a valuable hunter and a fierce fighter. Until the moment when everything had changed.

The tribe had tried to live, side by side, with the light-skinned. They had accepted the terms of peace in order to coexist in the unforgiving expanses of the plains. Then the white man had run out of resources to feed and shelter their kin and turned upon the peaceful tribe. They lost women and children. Their livestock was taken. The village burned. So the tribe defended its territory. They summoned the warrior spirit and attacked the settlement in a bloody fury. Crouching Bear had fought the raiding white man with his brothers. He had terrorized the men with collected scalps. He had stabbed a woman, round with an unborn child inside her. He slaughtered the white man's loyal dogs. And he had killed Laughing Crow, by accident.

Laughing Crow was the Chief's middle son. He was a fierce warrior and very strong. He was named for being an intelligent leader with a jovial sense of humor. Unlike most braves, he enjoyed the lighter side of life and shunned the seriousness of others. Laughing Crow was known to play tricks and he always had a funny story about emptying the anus. While many feared him, just as many followed him. But, on that day, his jokes had cost him his life.

Crouching Bear had just finished adding another scalp to his pouch when he noticed a man sneaking into one of the shelters. He followed the man inside and landed upon his back with his knife blade. The dead man hit the floor and Crouching Bear rolled him over to collect his token. That is when he learned that Laughing Crow had dressed himself in white-man's garments. Laughing Crow wore a heavy wool coat with a tan, felt hat. His hair was tucked inside the coat and all Crouching Bear saw was a man trying to escape. His last prank was the most costly.

In a panic, Crouching Bear tried to bring back Laughing Crow's warrior soul but it had already flown. Several tribesmen found him over the body and took him to the Chief. A hearing was held and Crouching Bear was banished from the tribe. Before they released him to the wilderness, he was cursed so that he and his future sons would always walk alone. A blood bounty was issued, and Crouching Bear knew more than a few warriors would seek him out, not only to avenge Laughing Crow's death, but also to elevate their status within the tribe.

He finally reached the tree line and discovered a game trail. It snaked to the left and then rose gradually through the forest. He would have to leave the game trail if he wanted to hide, but he knew the tracking skills of the men would lead them to the same conclusion. Crouching Bear found a thicket beneath a grove of spruce trees and settled down for a rest. The dappled sunlight cast shadows around the grove, providing more cover. He picked a few berries from his pouch and popped them into his mouth. The berries had soured and oozed juices on his fingers.

For the first time since the tribe had banished him, Crouching Bear was scared. He hadn't had any time to think or worry as he ran through endless fields. But now he replayed the tragedy in his mind. He felt the ground rumble with many feet searching for him. And he envisioned the slaughter that would arrive once they discovered him.

As he rested his legs, he thought about his parents and sister. He would never see them again and he left them in shame. They would now be labeled as the family of the one who killed Laughing Crow. While the tribe had no reason to blame them for his misdeeds, they would become outcasts just the same. Their future would be lonely and without pride.

A tear trickled down his darkened cheek like a mountain spring. It was so unfair that he could not speak for his mistake. The punishment was more than the crime. Laughing Crow's death was accidental. Banishment would have been a fitting price to pay. But cursing his soul and his future offspring's souls was a heavy price. Plus he must forever walk with silent steps so that the blood bounty would not follow him. There must be a place that he could escape to, where the tribe would eventually give up its search. If such a place existed, he must find it to survive.

He brushed the soil from his legs and began to pick his way through the dense forest. Every now and then, he would hide behind a tree or a rock to spy behind him. On one ridge, he carefully climbed a fir tree to gain a better vantage point from the treetops, using foliage for cover. There had been no signs of followers, yet. Crouching Bear expected that the men would use the opportunity to further hone their tracking skills. Giving him a head start was probably one of their tactics too. He figured they would want him to feel more comfortable and let his guard down so they could easily discover his mistakes. He knew he had to be sharper than them.

Crouching Bear rested against a stump. He tilted his face to the heavens and closed his eyes in prayer to the ancient ones. A twig snapped behind him and his eyes sprung open. He caught his breath and remained more still than a thousand year-old oak tree. A gentle crush of leaves and the slightest whisper of breathing carried to his ears. He silently looked over his right shoulder and a grizzled white man with a thick gray nest of beard stared at him. The white man had Crouching Bear in the iron sights of his rifle. Crouching Bear cursed himself for letting a white man sneak up on him. If he couldn't evade the white man, he stood no chance of surviving his tribesmen.

"Get up, yer beast. Nice and slow-like." He used the rifle to direct Crouching Bear to his feet. "Well, looky here. We got ourselves an Injun boy, eh?"

Crouching Bear stood still and looked over the man. The white man was older and probably too weak or slow to deal with him. However, he had the upper hand, at the moment, as he stared down the barrel of the gun.

"Whatcha got in yer pay-poose there, Chief? Anythings I could use or et?" The white man inched closer to Crouching Bear, who could now smell the man better than he could see him. The smell of urine and decaying meat drifted around the man. He spat in the dirt and inched even closer to Crouching Bear.

"Well, I guess the cat gotcher tongue er something but that don't bother me no-how. I aim to git what I came fer and nothin' else, so conversationalizing won't be necessary." The man squinted and reached slowly for Crouching Bear's pouch, one hand remained on the rifle with a finger on the trigger. As his dirty hand grabbed the pouch, Crouching Bear dropped to the dirt and swept the old-timer down with his leg. Before he could get his knife out, the white man had fired a shot at him. It missed Crouching Bear entirely but made him angrier than he had ever felt before. He knew the shot would signal the others to his location and that brought on an overwhelming rage.

Suddenly, Crouching Bear felt a tingle in his side and then it expanded into a burning pain, which reached over his chest, around his shoulder and down his spine. His neck stretched to the left and then to the right and he heard the sound of bones crunching. The old-timer watched on in horror as Crouching Bear's body began to change. He stripped off his garments as if his body was on fire. He felt heaviness filling his legs and hips while his chest expanded and grew hairy. His dark skin wrinkled and stretched as long, coarse hairs sprouted from every pore. Crouching Bear lost his thoughts as his head felt like thunder clouds hammering the silent morning. He dropped to his knees and his torso lengthened, doubling in size. The smell of the old man messing himself was pervasive, as it seemed he could now detect odors near and far with a heightened awareness. He roared and stood on his hind legs, towering eight feet above the white man lying on the ground.

In an instant, the monster that was Crouching Bear was upon the man. The old-timer tried to use the rifle as a wedge against the man-bear's jaws but it was no use. The man-bear swatted the rifle away like it was a piece of kindling. The beast sat on the man's chest, mauling his face and neck. It devoured the man's flesh like it hadn't eaten in days. It drank his blood, slaking its thirst from the long journey. The beast kept feeding, long after the old-timer ceased to be. The meal ended only when there was nothing left but bloody scraps and large bones.

Engorged, the man-bear licked its jowls and lay down in a thick patch of undergrowth. In between yawns, it slurped the last chunks stuck in its claws. The man-bear blinked slowly several times and then lowered its great head upon the earth. The beast snoozed with a full belly and a quiet mind.

Crouching Bear woke to the sound of a coyote howling in the darkness. The forest was black as pitch. His mouth tasted like blood. And his body felt small and very light. He sat naked on the ground, small sticks and leaves sticking to his skin. An overwhelming urge to void his bowels snapped him out of his sleep-induced fog.

The vision of his transformation floated before his eyes, a recounting of the whole event. The fire and the pain shooting through his body. His heightened sense of smell. The overwhelming desire to feed. The sound of the man's screams. Crouching Bear knew it was the curse. The tribe never said what kind of curse they had summoned upon him but it was clear they had created this monster. They had used his name against him. He was cursed to live out the essence of the wild bear. It confused him as to why the curse took hold when he came upon the old man. Why hadn't he turned into a bear while he was running through the fields? Or climbing up the trees? Or wading across a stream?

He fumbled along the ground in search of his garments. His hands scavenged through the soil, dirt accumulating beneath his fingernails. Crouching Bear found his clothes and began dressing when the urge to eliminate once again beckoned urgently. He squatted with his clothes balled up against his chest.

Moments later, Crouching Bear felt like a new man. He finished dressing himself, while he tried to figure out his next move.

CHAPTER 2

James whittled a stick out of boredom. He liked to keep his knife really sharp so the shavings of wood flaked off like shreds of cheese. As he worked the stick, James daydreamed of adventure. Like any other seventeen year old boy in a small, one-horse town, his future lie somewhere out in the wild. He thought this town was boring.

Life for James in Pella, Iowa revolved around working in the saloon all day and then avoiding the brothel upstairs each night. The repetitive cycle was endless but there was no escape. He lived upstairs in the brothel with his mother, so this was all he had.

"You're making a mess of the rug." George glared at him under the brim of his hat. James startled at the big man's intrusion. James knew better than to get on George's bad side. After all, he was the bouncer in the saloon downstairs. And James had seen George whip many a large dude who had misbehaved while tearing up the town. George brushed aside a long curl of his dark hair and spat a wad of chew. It missed the spittoon. He wiped some slick tobacco drool from his dark stubble.

"Sorry. I was just bored. I'll clean it up."

"Damn straight you'll clean it up. Ain't no customers gonna wait for a lady if the lounge is all dirty." George glanced at the splatter of missed tobacco on the carpet. "Best clean that up, too."

James rolled his eyes, in his mind. He wouldn't dare show disrespect, outwardly, to the bruiser. He didn't mind George's constant attitude but he didn't like it when George made a mess. George was deadly accurate with a six shooter but he was never accurate with his chaw. Never.

"Hello, George."

"Ma'am." George touched the brim of his hat and turned on his heels. He slowly walked down the wooden stairs to the bar.

"How are you today, darling?" James' mother, Sarah, bent to kiss his forehead. She ruffled his light brown hair. James thought she was the most beautiful woman in the whole world, let alone the brothel. Her long black hair juxtaposed her crystal blue eyes and fetched her a pretty penny since she looked different than all the other ladies. James had his father's coloring but he had inherited the same double dimples, on each side of his mouth, from his mother. "You better clean up this mess before Filler comes around. He'll be fit to be tied if he catches you making a mess on the rug."

"I know. I'll make sure everything is tidied up. Mom, I saw the paper this morning and father whooped another one. It said he clubbed the man with the butt of his gun again. People are talking that it is his signature move."

Sarah rested her hands on her hips and tsked. James knew it bothered her when he regaled his father's legends and exploits, but he couldn't help himself. He wanted to grow up to be a big, strong man like his father, the legendary Wyatt Earp. His father got to travel to different cities and fight bad guys and shoot up things. All the kinds of adventures James dreamed about.

"Now, James, you know I don't like it when you go around talking like that. Your daddy is not someone you should look up to. He can be a mean, self-centered bastard."

James lowered his head. He had heard this speech so many times before. He whittled a few more strokes and looked back at his mother. "Aw, mom. It's just that I'm bored being stuck in this town. Every day is the same and there's a whole world out there just waiting to be explored." He brushed a wisp of his light hair to the side, leaving a wood shaving behind. "I need adventure. I wanna rid the world of bad guys and be a hero. Not some bar sweep that lives with his momma."

Sarah smiled at James. She straightened the sleeves of her dress while carefully choosing her words. "I promise you, James. Someday you will be old enough to strike out on your own and see the world. But we just ain't got money enough for you to go off on a quest. And you are still too wet behind the ears to be on your own. There is a lot of danger out there and I can't hardly risk your precious soul to all that is bad in the world."

James stood and kicked at the pile of shavings on the rug. He stood slightly taller than his mother. Their eyes met and he read the worry in hers. He knew she could see the disappointment in his. But he couldn't hide his feelings. She had raised him to be an honest young man and he never lied. Truth was all he spoke, even when it would get him in trouble, like the time that Mr. Peters stole a bottle of rum when Filler wasn't looking. James told Filler and he had George put a whooping on Mr. Peters something serious. To this day, Mr. Peters was always very cold towards James. It bothered James because he wanted everyone to like him but he knew he did the right thing by tattling.

"James!" The distant hollering of Filler traveled up the stairs from the saloon. "Where is that confounding boy?"

Sarah licked her fingers and matted down a few stray hairs on the side of James' head. She plucked the errant shaving of wood out of his scalp and dropped it to the pile on the rug. "You best be getting downstairs before he bursts himself."

"But what about the wood shavings? George yelled at me to clean it up."

"I'll sweep it up. You get going before Filler comes upstairs." She brushed his shoulder to flatten a wrinkle in his shirt.

"Thanks, mom." He kissed her cheek and headed towards the staircase. Then he paused and turned. "Uh, George missed the spittoon again." He shrugged his shoulders in apology for getting away with another mess, even though he didn't make it. Sarah shook her head, in resignation, at adding to her chores. James smiled and went down the stairs.

As he started down, he overheard his mother sighing out loud to herself. "Such a sweet boy, and thank God he is nothing like his father."

"James!"

"Coming, Mr. Filler." He hurried down to the saloon.

CHAPTER 3

J ames finished wiping down all the tables and chairs in the saloon. The dull oak wood was stained with the aroma of wild nights. The smell of spilled beer and musty cigarettes permeated the first floor of the building. It used to disgust him to breathe in the stale air but after a few years he had become accustomed to it. His job was to clean up the previous night's remnants and then prepare the bar for the upcoming evening. It was a repetitive job that added to his frustration at the familiarity and further urged his longing for adventure.

He picked up the broom and started sweeping all the filth from under the tables. As he swept, along came his buddy, Carson, flying down the stairs. Carson looked excited to catch up with his "best friend in the whole wide world." That's what he called James. James liked spending time with Carson because he showed fascination at all of James' tales of adventures and shared his dreams of fighting bad guys. Carson was twelve years old and lived with his mother, in the brothel, just like James. The only difference, besides age, was that Carson was born with an illness which stunted his intellectual growth. He was slow and, when he had reached the age of five, his mother had pulled him out of school. She was afraid that it just brought Carson down not being able to keep up with the other children. Plus, she didn't like how the kids treated him. They knew he was not like them and they made him pay for it.

"James. James. Need help today?" Carson pleaded with wide blue eyes. He reached out a thin arm to take hold of the broom.

"No thanks, Carson. Filler is sore at me today so I don't want him getting madder if he catches you working with me." James stopped sweeping and looked around the bar to make sure the coast was clear. "Check this out. I tore this out of the morning paper on account that it was all read through and nobody else wanted it. Wyatt Earp did it again." He took a flimsy piece of newspaper out of his pocket and unfolded it in front of Carson. The boy's eyes grew wider and he leaned over the paper like it was a newborn in a crib. Carson couldn't read so James began to paraphrase the article while using his finger to point to sections.

"Oh, boy. He sure is gooder at taking care of business, huh, James?"

"Good." James corrected him. "He's good at taking care of business. Yeah, he sure is. I bet that rascal never saw it coming when Wyatt brought the butt down." James acted out the scene and the broom dropped to the floor. "Someday I'm gonna give it to them the same way. I'm going to clean the world of bad men, one town at a time."

"And you're gonna take me with you, right James?" The boy was beside himself with kaleidoscope eyes dreaming in his adventures. He still hadn't combed his hair from sleeping and a shock of blond hair stood straight up on the back of his head.

"You betcha." James patted Carson's shoulder and then picked up the broom. He continued to sweep, while spinning a tale of traveling and fighting and winning across the plains. Carson followed James closely, sometimes bumping into the back of James if he stopped short to sweep better under a table. James didn't mind at all. He loved Carson like a brother and kind of enjoyed the little guy looking up to him. Carson was all James had in this town. Well, he had his mother but she was always busy working and she didn't buy into his ambitions. Carson did. Carson would follow James anywhere.

George walked through the door and sauntered over to the bar, never once taking his dark eyes off the pair. The boys stopped and watched George. They were always unsure if they could carry on in his presence or if they should stay out of his way. Most times they would stay out of his way. George spat a wad of tobacco juice in the general direction of a spittoon but missed. As always. He licked the brown spittle from his lower lip and nodded down at the splatter on the pale wood floor.

"Supposing yer gonna need to clean that up." He stood straight up and adjusted his vest. George was extremely large. He was tall and full of muscles and most men turned the other way when George was in the area. He was good at his job of keeping the place under control. And everyone knew it. Except for the occasional drifter who had to learn the hard way.

"Whatter y'all standin' around for?" Filler lifted the counter and walked behind the bar. He had just come in from the back door. "I don't pay you to stand around gawking like a jaybird. And I certainly don't need you to be wasting my time with that retart." Filler was always ornery. James didn't especially like the bartender and owner. He was really skinny and had a pinched nose between beady eyes. Lots of lines wrinkled the sides of his eyes and waved across his forehead like an ocean.

"He ain't a retart. Don't call him that." James straightened his back and maintained strong eye contact with Filler. He found himself shocked that he had talked back to an adult, especially a grumpy adult who controlled his pay and his mother's job. But he never allowed people to get away with picking on Carson. In the past, it was always the children that he had dealt with. This time he was against a man.

"What didja say ta me?" Filler placed both hands upon the bar and leaned over in James' direction. He shot a glance at George, who smirked and then looked down at his boots. "You best mind yer manners, boy or I'll put a hurt on you that will land you in Doc's place." He pulled his handlebar mustache out to the side.

"Yes, sir. I'm sorry. I just get madder than a badger when somebody does harm to Carson." James glanced at Carson, who was standing with his hands on his hips in defiance of Filler.

"Well, I'll let 'er slide this time but you get back to fixing things up and get that boy back to his mama. The saloon ain't no place for a baby to be moseying about." Filler picked up a mug and spat into it then stuffed a rag to the bottom and twisted. He stormed out the back door in a huff. James just looked down at Carson and ruffled his hair. Carson beamed up at his hero. George walked over and towered over the boys.

"You got stones, kid." George winked at James and then went out the swinging front doors.

James looked around and the boys were alone again.

"Don't think nothing of it, Carson. We won't have to deal with this much longer. Real soon, we're gonna walk on out and get ourselves some adventure. If the criminals were smart, they'd start running now, before we get started." He smiled confidently and started sweeping again. "But first I gotta work."

"Back to square one." Carson followed James as he worked.

CHAPTER 4

"How do you do it? You win every time we play." James had gotten better at playing cards but not good enough to whip Carson. Carson was something of an expert and he never got tired of winning. In a world where Carson seemed to lose at everything else, this was fine by James. He tried to learn all he could from playing with Carson. He envisioned himself beating a card shark, in a game of five card stud, sending the conman packing.

"It's not magic, James." Carson looked up at him and blinked profusely. "You just have to pay attention." He rubbed his small fist across his mouth to remove some invisible tickle.

"But I do pay attention. I always pay attention."

Carson giggled and collected the cards again. He started to shuffle the cards, his hands moving adeptly like a seasoned dealer. While he studied Carson's hands, James continued to share his fantasies.

"Just think what we could do out there. Gamblers scamming people out of their hard-earned money and then we sit at the table. The crowd would gather around, hanging on every card as it's put down. The women gasping and the men wishing they was us. Then we scoop up the money and go have a time or two, doing whatever we want. That would be something, huh, buddy?"

The younger boy kept shuffling with a wide grin on his dirty face.

"And then we wouldn't have to sit outside every night while the adults carried on like they do." James turned his head so that his ear faced the back door to the saloon. Loud roars of laughter and shouting beat against the closed door.

As with everything else, James had grown tired of this same routine every night. They were the only youngsters who lived in the brothel so they had to stay out all night until the parties died down. Most nights the boys played cards until 3 or 4 a.m. before either falling asleep on the back porch or walking to their favorite "hiding spot." The hiding spot was a great place to not only hide but also to catch some sleep. They had discovered the spot one summer afternoon when they went exploring just outside of town. In a wooded lot nearby, there was a gully and at the bottom of the gully was a huge, tangled tree root exposed above the surface. The boys burrowed a nest of sorts beneath the roots and they planted lots of chickweed around the roots. The growth formed a thick green cover to further hide their location. Every few months, the boys would line the earth below with squares of moss so they had nice, cushy and cool bedding.

James turned his attention back to Carson who was dealing out another hand.

"I like sitting outside every night. My mom said that only big boys get to stay out late so that means I'm fine." His tongue jetted out to hold his upper lip up while he finished dealing.

"No, that means you're fine with it, not you're fine. Anyways, I like to play cards with you so I guess it ain't all that bad." James picked up his cards and frowned at the hand he was dealt. He looked over at Carson, who was smiling back at him.

"What's the big idea?"

"You aren't paying attention and it's funny." Carson put a hand over his mouth and giggled. Then he looked back at his own hand with serious concentration.

"Am too paying attention. I paid so much attention I'm getting all the worst cards. That must be how you beat me all the time." James furrowed his eyebrows and leaned toward Carson. "If I didn't know any better, I would say you was cheating. But I ain't saying that on account of you being my friend and on another account of I wouldn't want to make you sore for accusing you of such."

The show of respect elicited another giggle from Carson, as he felt James was afraid of him dishing out a beating on the much bigger boy.

"Now…pay…attention." Carson ordered James with strong emphasis on each word.

The boys went through the cards without a word. Each boy raised the other by adding a few buttons to the pile. Carson called. James laid down two pairs. Carson beamed as he laid down a full house. James scratched his head and looked at the cards and then at Carson and back down at the cards again. He whistled.

"I'll be."

"I told you to pay attention."

"I did pay attention, dang it."

"No, you didn't." He smiled.

"Just deal another round so I can learn more." James exhaled some frustration.

Carson started shuffling the deck. "Back to square one."

CHAPTER 5

James scooped another heaping spoonful of scrambled eggs into his mouth. He loved breakfast because it was the only meal of the day when he got to sit at a table and eat like a normal person. Lunch was always served while he worked in the saloon and dinner was eaten on the back porch, well out of the way of "paying customers." Filler was clear about his priorities and profit was right up there at the top of the list. Feeding James and Carson was an added expense that he begrudgingly accepted, only because Sarah and Minnie, James' and Carson's mothers respectively, were two of his best earners.

Carson forked around his eggs without any intention of eating. His eyes were half-closed and he yawned as he leaned his head on one elbow. Carson was not a morning person and he usually passed up breakfast. Today he had accepted it but continued to play with his food.

James looked at Carson's plate with a huge lump of eggs in his cheek. He chewed and looked down at his plate. "You gonna eat those eggs?"

Carson opened one sleepy eye and shook his head no to James. He put the fork down and pushed his plate across the table. With no hesitation, James lifted the plate and funneled the food onto his own. A mountain of eggs sat in the middle of the dish, some spilling over onto his bacon.

"Thanks." James smiled at his windfall. He scooped another large mouthful and shoveled it in. "I wonder if Wyatt made the news again today. We should git over to the barber shop to scrounge for used papers." He chewed, paused for a burp and then continued chewing.

"Okay." Carson was clearly not enthusiastic yet.

A loud yell carried in through the swinging doors of the saloon. Apparently, somebody in the street was angry and was taking it out on another citizen. The yelling quickly turned into a roar as the sound of a crowd raised the noise level. James dropped his fork in mid-chew and pushed back his chair. Carson's eyes finally opened wide and he followed James to the door.

In the street, a few yards from the saloon, a crowd of about ten people formed a circle around two men in a dispute. One man was the town drunk, Wilson. The other man was an Indian. James looked down at Carson, who returned his glance. Both boys pushed through the swinging doors and approached the crowd. James politely squeezed in between a few onlookers. Carson just brushed his way through without awareness that he had elbowed one man and stepped on another's boot.

"Ain't no place fer Injuns here, man. Best be on yer way 'afore I give you a whatfor. Now sket atta here." Wilson wobbled upon his non-stop drunken legs. He was drunk at all times of the day even though he only drank at night. Folks knew he put down enough whiskey each night to keep himself in a constant state of inebriation.

The Indian glared at Wilson in silence. He shifted on his feet to take inventory of the crowd and the circle which seemed to be closing in on him. But he stood his ground in defiance. It was clear he wasn't going to run.

"I said git a mosey on, ya red-bellied heathen. Er I'm gonna paint yer nose with yer blood, boy." Wilson put up his fists and teetered left, caught himself, and then faltered back a few steps. The crowd shifted around Wilson, allowing him room to get settled.

James overheard one man tell another that the Indian had wandered into town and Wilson had stopped him before he started any trouble. James didn't think the Indian was looking for trouble. For one thing, he was alone so he wasn't coming to raid the town. For another, he didn't appear to have any weapons so it was clear he was in need of help. No

Indian in his right mind would stroll into a settled town, alone and unarmed, unless he was itching to be corralled and tossed in the jail.

James stepped into the circle. "Hey, wait a minute." He surprised himself that he took center stage. "Can't you see he ain't got no guns and he's alone? Why would he come here like that if he was aiming to start trouble?" James' questions spurred a fresh uproar and one man shoved James in the chest. The crowd wanted blood and they were in Wilson's corner.

Wilson leaned into James and breathed whiskey breath into his face. James' eyes watered and he coughed, as he swallowed hard to gasp for fresh air. "Ain't no place fer a boy ta stick his'n nose where it ain't berlong. Mebbe I should teach ya a lesson with this here Injun."

James pushed Wilson aside. The crowd immediately stopped shouting, shocked by the young man's bravery. James was surprised himself but couldn't stop the train from rolling now that it was moving. "Don't call me a boy, Wilson. And this Indian ain't doing nothing wrong. So back off before I get George out here." The crowd shifted uneasily. "I know you don't want George to clean up yer mess."

Wilson staggered back and forth, blood lust danced in his hazel eyes. His overly-wild eyebrows skittered up and down, as he worked hard to get his temper under control. A bead of sweat shone on his bushy mustache. "I ain't gonna fergit this'n here tribulation. You better watch yer back when I come near."

"What are you gonna do? Drink me under the table?" James sassed Wilson and the crowd roared with laughter. The heaviness in the air flew away as the men enjoyed the joke at Wilson's expense. One man clapped Wilson on the back while he laughed and another guy led Wilson across the street to the mercantile. The mob dispersed and the Indian looked around in amazement that he had just dodged a bullet.

Carson was awestruck and smiled up at James. James just looked at the Indian, who returned the stare. "You're a hero, James. You did it."

James ignored Carson's praise and took a few steps toward the Indian. The Indian approached and nodded his appreciation. James nodded back and wondered what had brought the man to town.

"I'm James. This is Carson. Do you need help or something?"

The Indian stared at James for several moments and then nodded again. James breathed a sigh of relief that he had done the right thing in saving the man from certain trouble.

"We got some breakfast inside if you wanna eat. Won't be no trouble to give you some." James waited for the Indian to acknowledge his offer but the Indian remained stoic. "Well, come on then." James indicated that the man should follow them into the saloon. As they started for the doors, James looked over his shoulder to find the man following along. He smiled down at Carson, who beamed at the adventure they had just had. Both boys were satisfied that the day held more promise than usual.

CHAPTER 6

James and Carson burst into the lounge with excitement. Carson was holding a dead rabbit in his hands, the long gray ears dangled to the floor. Sarah and Minnie were sweeping the rugs and wiping down the small bar. A few of the other working girls were fluffing the couch cushions and dusting the light fixtures.

Sarah saw the boys first. "Well, what do we have here?" She poked Minnie to get her attention. Minnie spun around and grimaced at the dead animal.

"We saved an Innian man and feeded him and then went hunting and catched a bunny, with his help, and we played in the fields and came back." Carson blurted everything out in one breathless rant. His desire to be the first one to recount the story caused him to misstate what he had really intended to say.

"You what?" Minnie crouched down to look her son in the eyes. She looked him over in her usual over-protective manner to be sure the boy wasn't bruised or injured. She could never control herself because she was always worried for her simple child.

James jumped in to clear up the confusion. "An Indian came to town this morning. His name is Crouching Bear and he was kicked out of his tribe and had nowhere to go. He happened by town and decided to stop in." James looked down at Carson, who nodded in confirmation. "Wilson and some ruffians was gonna hurt him so, Carson and me, we brought him in and gave him breakfast. We talked about adventures and he said he could show us a better way to catch rabbits. So we went hunting with him and he taught us a fool-proof trapping technique." James was the one speaking without breathing now. He paused to gasp for air.

Sarah took advantage of the pause to jump in. "And where is this Indian friend of yours now?" She worriedly looked behind the boys to see if the man was inside.

"His name is Crouching Bear. And we left him outside town in the woods. He was afraid to come back into town lest Wilson and the others give him a hard time again."

"Well, that's good. You know how Filler feels about Indians. And George too. It wouldn't be a good idea to bring someone like that around here."

"Aw, he's okay. He is big and strong." Carson added his input.

"Big and strong, huh? Sounds like a nice man." Minnie winked at Sarah in a flirtatious display of the possibilities. She enjoyed her job very much. Sarah rolled her eyes at Minnie. Carson was oblivious to her comment and James chose not think about it.

"Yeah, and there was a misunderstanding with his elders and he got blamed for some accident. So they cursed him and his whole family." James screwed up his face. "Now he is lonely and has nowhere to go. And he told us that the tribe wants to kill him so he is trying to find somewhere to live without them finding him. He figured the tribe wouldn't come into a town unless they wanted to start a war. But now with Wilson…" He trailed off, as he struggled to think of options for his new friend.

Sarah and Minnie exchanged glances as they could see the boys were worried about the Indian. Sarah thought for a moment and then offered her idea. "Maybe we can work out a way that he can help out here in the saloon." The boys looked up in excitement but Sarah put them in their places before they could get any wild ideas with her suggestion. "But that will take some time. We will have to use our womanly skills to persuade

Filler. And George won't like the idea. It won't be easy and it may not be possible at all."

Carson was visibly deflated. James, his shoulders slumped, knew it would be almost impossible for them to convince Filler.

"I think you should bring that rabbit back to him so he has something to eat in the meantime."

Minnie grimaced at the animal again. "I'd sure like to meet him. I don't know how comfortable I am to have a strange man going around with my precious little boy. And a dangerous Indian to boot. But we won't have time to leave town to see him. And Filler won't let us wander that far off anyway. Maybe the boys can sneak him inside for a few minutes so we can look him over."

Carson's face lit up again. James nodded. "We can sneak him in. We can do anything. It'll be an awesome adventure."

Sarah shook her head at her son's endless attempts to create "adventures." "I don't know. Should we risk our livelihood before we have a chance to slowly work on Filler?"

"So you're okay with a strange Indian going around with the boys?" Minnie pleaded with Sarah.

"I guess not. I mean I do trust James' judgment but I would feel better if I could meet the man." Sarah thought it over for a second. "Alright. But you boys have to make sure Filler and George do not find out about this. They won't be happy about this and might kick us out. Then where would we go?"

James already had a plan figured out. "It'll be easy. All we have to do is wait for the beginning of the night when things get busy, but not so busy that lots of people will see." James rubbed his hands together. "We can sneak him in the back door and run him upstairs before customers come up."

The mothers relented and agreed to the plan. The boys ran downstairs to hurry up with the cleaning duties so they could get back out to the woods. James wouldn't be allowed to do anything until his responsibilities were handled. And Carson had to follow close behind James like a shadow. Sarah grinned at Minnie.

The ladies returned to their own cleaning tasks. Minnie paused for a moment and stared off, imagining something. Sarah noticed and cleared her throat to get Minnie refocused on cleaning. Minnie smiled at Sarah.

"You know, I've never had an Indian." Sarah rolled her eyes again. "It would be nice to know what it's like to be with a savage."

"You would lie with anyone, wouldn't you?"

"Not just anyone. But you can't say you aren't curious about what it must be like to be taken by a wild man. The strength and the power would be wonderful. Not like all these flabby old has-beens that come up." Minnie continued to imagine the possibilities.

Sarah chuckled. "It might be different. But those flabby old has-beens keep money in our purses. An Indian wouldn't be a paying customer."

Minnie laughed out loud. "Consider it charity then, just one human being helping out another." She bit her lower lip and continued cleaning.

"Ugh. You are a unique one, Minnie. You really are." Sarah giggled and then both of them laughed.

CHAPTER 7

J ames and Carson made sure to make enough noise as they approached their hiding spot. James didn't want to surprise Crouching Bear and find himself on the sharp end of a knife or anything. James figured, even if they crept in carefully, Crouching Bear would know it. When he showed them how to snare the rabbit earlier, he had displayed such amazing body control and stealth that James was envious. He paid attention to each movement as he studied the Indian. In James' mind, there was no better way to prepare for an adventure than to study from an expert of the wilderness.

Crouching Bear stuck his head out from under the gnarled roots of the tree. He had covered his face with dirt and bits of moss so he blended in with his environment. But James knew where he was so it was easy enough to pick out the blinking eyes. James made another mental note on how to better hide using the Indian's tactics.

"Howdy."

Crouching Bear nodded imperceptibly and then crawled out of the hollow. He looked at the boys and then surveyed the area to see if they had betrayed him, bringing men from the town with them. James caught this and reassured Crouching Bear.

"It's just us. We wouldn't bring anyone else." Crouching Bear relaxed. "Besides, this is our secret hiding spot. We would never tell anyone where this spot is because then we wouldn't have a place to go. 'Cept you. You're our friend, right?" Crouching Bear didn't react, still unsure if he could trust any white man.

"We speaked to our moms and they said we should bring you home." Carson blurted out.

"We spoke, Carson, spoke. Anyway, our mothers would like to meet you, if you are okay coming with us back to town."

Crouching Bear tensed again. He squatted down on his haunches and started skinning the rabbit the boys had brought back. James watched in amazement at how quickly the man unsheathed his knife and went to work on the carcass. In a matter of moments, the rabbit was skinned, gutted and filleted. James scorned himself at his lack of awareness that the Indian was hiding a weapon. It briefly occurred to him that he and Carson could have been killed. He would have to pay more attention to people in the future or else his adventures would end quickly and painfully. He was also a little angry with himself for putting Carson in harm's way. He could deal with risking his own neck but not the little boy.

Crouching Bear tossed a severed rabbit's foot to each boy. Carson let out a loud "wow" and turned the foot over in his small hands, inspecting it and petting the soft fur. James looked at the foot with wonder and smiled at the man. For the first time, Crouching Bear smiled back at him. James warmed instantly, feeling that he was breaking through the rugged exterior of the man.

"So you should eat the rabbit and then we will come back for you later, when the time is right for sneaking you into the bar."

The Indian shook his head no and then stroked James' cheek with two fingers. The rabbit blood painted two stripes down his face. He repeated the process on the other side. James was taken aback by the gesture but tried not to show that he was startled. He didn't want to frighten the man. Then he smiled, figuring that Crouching Bear was initiating him with some ritual or another.

"Me too. Me too." Carson jumped forward and leaned down into Crouching Bear's personal space. James smiled, and then giggled. Crouching Bear studied James' reaction and then smiled again. He dabbed his fingers into the pile and put fresh stripes on Carson's cheeks. Carson was beside himself with delight. "Oh boy."

"I will not go to town with you." Crouching Bear spoke solemnly. "Not welcome in white man's world."

"Hogwash." James responded. "We have a plan all figured out to get you in without anyone noticing. Once we get you in the back door, it will be easy. You'll see." James tried to reassure the man with his expression, as well as his words.

"Please come home with us, Mr. Bear. Please." Carson did his best to cajole the Indian. He used the same expression and tone that worked on his mother when he really wanted to get his way.

Crouching Bear picked up on the little boy's desperation and found it hard to ignore. "Not good idea to tempt the spirits."

"But we promise it will all work out. Otherwise, our mothers won't let us see you anymore. You have to meet them so we can stay friends. Won't you please come to town? We can get you more food to eat, too. You can share our supper with us." James tried to throw in a bonus to sweeten the deal.

Crouching Bear gave up. He looked at each boy and then nodded. Carson jumped up and down in elation. James sighed with relief and smiled. He reached out to shake Crouching Bear's hand. Crouching Bear looked down at James' hand and then accepted the gesture. They shook hands and James felt the overwhelming power of the Indian's grip. He had instant visions of the man fighting off whole tribes of men with such strength. He couldn't help but wonder if the Indian would someday join him and Carson on their adventures. They could certainly use his skills and knowledge. And, with that strength, they would be a formidable team.

James stood up and brushed the dust off his dungarees. Carson stopped hopping around and imitated James. He stood at attention alongside James. Crouching Bear saw the admiration and stood up himself. The gesture further bonded the three. James put his arm around Carson and pulled him into his side with brotherly affection.

"We'll be back to get you just before sundown. Then we'll introduce you to our mothers. And we can have supper and play cards. It'll be fun."

Crouching Bear nodded and the boys turned to head back to town. Crouching Bear watched them go, the little one danced as he walked alongside the older one. He began to wonder if his feelings towards white men were wrong. He had never had good experiences with the pale face people but these two boys had stirred something inside of him he had not felt before.

CHAPTER 8

"Okay, you ready?" James prepared Crouching Bear to enter the saloon through the back door. After finishing his job late in the afternoon, James took Carson back out to the hiding spot to pick up Crouching Bear. Unlike last time, the Indian was sitting outside the hollow on a stump. He appeared to be sleeping in the seated position but James realized he must have been praying to his spirits or thinking about his family. The boys had little trouble convincing him to follow them back to town. The man apparently had made his peace with the decision.

James brought Crouching Bear a hat and an old leather duster that had been left in the saloon a long time ago. Nobody had ever come back to claim it so the coat just gathered dust, wadded in a ball, in the back of the broom closet. James helped the Indian stuff his long black hair up under the hat so he wouldn't look so obvious. The leather duster extended down to his knees, further hiding his tribal apparel. James figured that few people, if any, would glance down at the man's footwear to notice his moccasins.

Crouching Bear nodded and James took a deep breath. He had just reached for the back door to the saloon when it thumped into his face and knocked him back into Crouching Bear. Carson, too little to see what was coming ahead of him, walked right into the rump of the Indian before plopping down on the porch boards. George darkened the doorway and stifled a curse word as he saw who took the brunt of the door.

"Whatcha doing with yer face on the door, kid?" His attitude was consistent, if not apologetic. George's eyes lifted from James' face to the big man standing behind him. He squinted as he tried to make out the features on Crouching Bear, who kept his head tilted down so that the brim of the hat shielded his face. "Well, what do we have here?"

James panicked and stammered, trying to cover up their unwelcome friend. "What? Him? Oh, uh, he's just somebody we bumped into. He, um, said he was lost and thirsty so we brought him over to get a drink, that's all." James had never lied in his life and he looked down at his boots in guilt. Sure he had told tiny white lies or half-truths but he had never told an out and out lie like this before. Then again, he thought, he had never really done anything so bad as to require such a bold-faced lie.

George didn't buy it. He moved James aside with hardly a finger and then stood toe to toe with the stranger. George waited a long few seconds for the man to look up into his face before he realized he wouldn't. George slowly lifted the brim of the hat with his index finger, his eyes opening wider when he saw the face. "I knew you was up to no good, James, when I seen yer hat on his head." George shifted his attention to James. "An Injun, James? Of all the folks you hustle in here, you bring one of them?" George turned his glare back to Crouching Bear's face. Crouching Bear returned the gaze without flinching. James noticed that, for once, there was somebody in town who was as big as George.

"Look, he's our friend. We saved him from Wilson and the ruffians this morning and our mothers wanted to meet him on account of what happened is all. He's just going to come upstairs with us and then we'll bring him back. Honest."

"Yeah, I heard about yer little grandstand today." George turned his head and spat tobacco juice over the railing. He left the drool on his dark whiskers. "You seemed to be all growed up lately, James. First Filler, then the townsmen. Shit, I ain't take offense with yer lip to Wilson. He ain't nothing but a cow-turd anyhow. But yer starting to play games with the big boys now." He spat again, never breaking eye contact with Crouching Bear.

"My mom said it was okay to bring him just for a minute, okay? So that's all we're gonna do." James was scrambling for what other fuel he could use to slip the Indian by George.

"Wonder what Filler would have to say about this'n here?" He looked at James. James glanced at Carson who was hiding behind Crouching Bear. He was at a loss for words and wondered if he would pee himself soon. "But I ain't no rat. And I'm in a forgiving mood at this time of the night. But I'll be watching the stairs fer him to git on outta here in short order."

James looked up in relief. "Thanks, George. I promise, we'll have him out in no time. You'll see." James started to reach for the door to the saloon but George grabbed his arm and pulled him close, while maintaining eye contact with Crouching Bear. "Just know this. I don't like his kind. And, if I catch wind he's so much as blinked the wrong way, then he will have to answer to me die-rectly." He grinned widely into Crouching Bear's face. Then let go of James' arm. Without waiting further, James yanked the back door open and ushered Crouching Bear inside. Carson hurried behind, holding onto James' belt loop. The door slammed shut behind them.

George stared off at the moon rising over the prairie. He breathed in the fresh night air and rubbed his stubble. "I'm sure we'll be seeing each other again, Mr. Injun." He looked around the porch and then returned to the saloon, eagerly anticipating having to tangle with the big Indian at a point later in the night.

"My, oh my. Ain't you a big man?" Minnie sidled up to the stranger who stood rigid before the ladies. She checked him out from top to bottom. Sarah, seeing her best friend sizing up the groceries, decided to intervene.

"Hello. I'm Sarah Johnson. I'm James' mother." She offered her hand to Crouching Bear, who looked down at it momentarily and then squeezed it hard. Sarah winced but tried not to yank her hand back.

"This is Minnie. She is Carson's mother." Sarah glanced nervously at Minnie, who circled Crouching Bear. She shot a look at James, who awkwardly looked down at his boots. Carson remained slightly hidden behind James, somewhat unsure of the encounter.

Crouching Bear settled his gaze upon Minnie, who clearly liked what she saw.

"Um, well, okay. I guess now that you've met him, we should be getting him outside." James started to indicate it was time to leave.

"Now what's the rush, sweetie? We got all night to talk. And do other fun things." Minnie smiled and bit her lower lip. She ran a finger down the man's chest. Crouching Bear seemed confused but quickly caught on to the game.

"We, sort of, got caught bringing him in here." James admitted, while shrugging his shoulders in guilt.

"What? I told you to be careful. What happened?" Sarah showed her concern for her livelihood.

"George walked up on us and we couldn't get by without him questioning us."

"Tsk. I don't know who's worse, George or Filler. They're both grumpier than a pack mule at high noon." Sarah shook her head, wondering what might befall them now.

"He said he wouldn't tell on us if we moved quickly and got him out of here." James assured the ladies. "So we'll just be on our way and nobody will be the wiser."

"Hold up, young man." Minnie hooked her arm in Crouching Bear's. "I'd like to show this gentleman around a bit and then I will personally see that he leaves without trouble."

"But what about George? He'll pound us fer sure." James was frightened of not keeping his end of the agreement. He felt Carson completely bury his face in his backside.

Minnie chuckled. "You leave George to me. He won't mind when I talk to him...alone." She started to lead Crouching Bear toward the rooms. James watched, with his mouth opened wide, unsure of what to do next. Sarah chewed her fingernail and then put her hand on his shoulder.

"I know this is scary but we'll work it out. You better be on your way before Filler catches you boys upstairs during work hours. His mustache will droop further down his face if he finds you here." She patted down some loose hairs on the side of his head and spun him toward the staircase.

James obeyed his mother's instructions but he had a huge pit in his stomach. The best day of his life was taking a nosedive. It started with an exciting adventure and he thought it was going to end with his death, or at least a hide skinning like none other. The boys shuffled down the stairs.

Sarah watched them go down the stairs and then turned to see where Minnie had gone. The Indian and her best friend were gone.

CHAPTER 9

Carson shuffled the deck with adept hands. His tongue touched his upper lip as he focused on the task. James threw pebbles off the back porch of the saloon. He didn't see where they landed because night had already settled upon the town. The roar of laughter and glasses clinking together sounded from inside the door.

"I'm so sick of this place." James threw another pebble. "All that ever happens is working and sitting. Sitting and working. And I'm tired of getting yelled at too." He nodded towards the bar even though Carson was looking down. "It's only fixing to get worse once George finds out we left Crouching Bear upstairs."

Carson dealt the hand. He blinked rapidly as he spoke to James. "Neat how we snucked outta there before he seen us. We tricked him good."

"We snuck, not snucked. Anyways, it won't be long before he gets wise to what we did." He picked up his hand and looked it over. He sat up straight when he realized he finally had a good hand. Suddenly, the possibility of beating Carson at cards took the frustration out of his mood.

Carson watched James and inventoried his own hand. His face remained expressionless. James looked, over his cards, at Carson, tapping his foot contentedly on the boards. Both boys anted up and raised each other several buttons before calling. James plunked his straight down with exuberance and leered at Carson with victorious satisfaction. Carson noted his excitement and carefully laid his hand on top of James'. Full house, yet again.

"Dang it!" James kicked the cards off the porch. His friend smiled quietly and began gathering the cards up from the dirt. "I ain't never gonna win a game."

Carson kept picking up cards and stacking them in his small fist. "You didn't pay attention."

Just as James was about to respond with a wisecrack, a crash came from the bar. Several women screamed and the sound of tables and chairs scraping along the wood floor wafted outside. The boys heard George curse a few times in between the sound of punches connecting. A few moments later the crowd cheered and the piano started playing again. Saloon life had returned to normal after George had taken care of the situation.

Carson waited for James to turn back to him; then he began dealing another hand. James didn't want to play cards anymore. He told Carson to put away the cards and the friends sat in silence for a while, watching the stars and moon high above the town. James daydreamed about striking out on his own and living in different towns like his father. He pictured himself hammering the butt end of his revolver on many black-hatted heads. He saw people admiring him as he strolled down the streets. He smelled the perfume of the most beautiful women, who all doted on him. It would be great to be the hero and have newspapers write about his deeds.

The back door swung open and the heavy footfalls of a drunken customer startled the boys out of their thoughts. They turned just in time to avoid Wilson, the town drunk, stepping on them as he faltered forward. The man missed the wooden steps and plunged to the dirt below, face first. James and Carson exchanged glances. Wilson rolled over, his tan hat brim dented and his cigar crumpled up in his teeth. Oddly enough, a fraction of the lit end still smoldered, even though it was off to the side of the rest of the cigar. Wilson managed to sit up and he puffed away to re-fire the smoke, while he dusted off his hat. "I musta got turned around there, fellas." He was in much better spirits, at the moment, than he had been this morning when James stood up to him. James prepared himself for Wilson to give him grief but it seemed the drunk had forgotten all about the morning incident. "Well don't jest set there a'lookin' inta the sky, will ya? Hep a good man up, now, see?" Wilson extended his hands for assistance.

James was relieved Wilson wasn't going to mention the argument. He hopped down off the porch and picked up the drunken townsman. The smell of tobacco and whiskey permeated the surrounding region and James fought hard to get fresh air. He stood Wilson up. Wilson teetered to the left and then stumbled back to the right before gaining a solid foothold. His boots were all scuffed from falling down and dragging his heels all the time. He patted the dust off his jacket, clouds of particles floated into the night. James turned and saw Carson sitting on the porch watching the whole show go down. The boy giggled and James started to snicker, himself, when the door swung open once more.

Filler cowered in the doorway with his pinched nose and hawk-like, beady eyes. He observed the boys staring at Wilson and that was all it took to set him off. "What in hell blazes are ya doing out here? You boys bothering my customers?" He yelled at them, in general, but James knew it was directed at him.

"No, sir. Mr. Wilson just stepped outside for a moment. He got confused and thought the back door was the front door."

"Well, that ain't make no sense, boy. Anyone can see the front doors is swinging in the breeze and the back door is solider than stone." He shot a look at Wilson. "Even Wilson can tell that difference."

James looked down at his boots and thought to himself that apparently Wilson couldn't tell the difference. But he kept his sass inside. Carson had crawled under the wooden steps to the porch without anybody noticing. He cowered beneath the porch, his eyes pleading to James to finish the scene. James tapped his fingers along his leg to signal Carson that everything would be fine.

"Wilson, you git yer pickled ass back inside er get gone right now. I ain't runnin no sideshow here." Filler stormed back into the bar and slammed the door shut. He re-opened the door once he remembered why he had come out back in the first place. He splashed the filthy bucket of water over the porch. It smelled of soap suds mixed with whiskey and vomit. The bucket dripped on the floor and Filler slammed the door shut again. James went back to the porch and sat on the steps. Carson crawled around the steps and sat in between James' legs.

Wilson wobbled on his feet while trying to figure out his next move. His wild eyebrows shifted up and down in opposite direction of his teetering stance. It appeared that a good idea had come to him and then he shuffled off into the dark. His direction wasn't aimed at the saloon or the side street. It was more or less diagonal to the row of buildings. The boys watched Wilson, silently guessing where he was headed.

"Let's go somewhere, Carson. I'm done sitting on this porch for tonight."

"Okay. Carson stood before James did. He grabbed James' belt loop and James put his arm around Carson's shoulders. They walked slowly toward their hiding spot, all the while laying out their plans for leaving this life for one of adventure, fighting the evils of the world.

CHAPTER 10

Crouching Bear sat in a wooden rocking chair, while Minnie blew out a few candles. The shadowy room got noticeably darker, but was light enough for him to see the beautiful white woman. He admired the silky glow of her light skin and the delicate curves of her soft body. Crouching Bear had known the pleasures of the flesh before. All warriors were initiated into manhood by tribe women set aside for just such times. And he had taken a white woman once before, during a war party. The warriors had raided a village of white men who had taken land from them. He had experienced everything that night in true warrior fashion. Killing, scalping, raping and then burning the huts and stealing the livestock. It had been a victorious night. But those women were hard and big, like men. Tribe women and peasant whites were not delicate. They were not small. They were not graceful.

Minnie frolicked and danced before him. She caressed her neck and shoulders with a feather boa, writhing in the flickering light. Her shadow danced upon the walls with a slight delay. She giggled and cooed, teasing the large Indian with her display of sexuality.

Crouching Bear felt his loins rise with heat. He thought to himself that he had never felt as large and full as he did now. His mind was furiously anticipating the warmth of the woman, the smell of her musk and the deepness of the coming oneness. He started to rise but Minnie shoved him back down. She knelt before him and massaged him with skill that he had not known, her hot breath upon his skin, sending tingles from his groin to his toes.

Not being able to withstand the seduction any longer, Crouching Bear lifted Minnie with one hand like she was a small child. He pulled her into his muscular chest with thick arms and large hands. He took two steps across the small room and then plunged into her as he landed on her bed. He entered easily, as she had anticipated his touch too. He trembled and penetrated repeatedly while Minnie squeezed the brass rails behind her. She accepted the largeness and he felt her pleasure. He grunted as he raised himself on solid arms and continued to glide on his white princess. Her soft belly kissed his hard stomach over and over. Crouching Bear closed his eyes and buried his head in her shoulder, concentrating on the sensations, with every fiber of his being.

Minnie cried out in ecstasy, grasping the brass rails. She lifted her hips to meet his thrusts and she swiveled in circles coaxing his pleasure further. Her breasts trembled with each penetration and brushed against the stone chest of the Indian. Both bodies moist, sweating and slipping with passion. Her cries interspersed with moans, the pace quickening. She clutched his buttocks and focused her eyes on the ceiling. The cords in her neck were straining to break free. He grunted and went deeper, faster. The bed shifted on the wood floor and smacked against the outside wall. The momentum increased and then exploded.

Crouching Bear shivered and trembled as he settled inside her. His whole spirit lost in a moment of time with no substance, no reality. Just an essence, a fleeting chasm in the universe, without boundaries. He knew that this was the most alive he had ever felt. His head sunk further into the pillow and he tried to slow his breathing.

Minnie giggled softly, holding the large man to her skin. She wiggled gently to keep his flagging spirit from withering. She sighed and closed her eyes contentedly.

Crouching Bear opened his eyes in a drowsy haze. The room had gotten darker as one of the lit candles had burned to the bottom. Minnie was dressing on the other side of the room. She patted a talcum with a flowery scent across her breasts and between her legs. He stretched his arms behind his head as he watched her delicate shape. Minnie heard him stir and glanced toward the bed. She took notice of the largeness which had already reappeared.

"Did you have a nice time?" She tucked her breasts in a bodice of black lace. Minnie wiggled her backside at him in a taunting display of naughtiness.

Crouching Bear nodded. He hoped she would return to the bed so he could soar with the spirits once more.

Minnie walked up to the bed and plopped down next to him. She stroked his stomach. "I never had a red man before. It's nice to finally get a chance to feel the wild side." She giggled. "Of course, I would lose all my clients if they knew I had been with a savage." She stared at the ceiling to think further about that. "At the least, I would have to charge on discount."

Crouching Bear stiffened at her harsh words. He was shocked that something so soft and beautiful could turn so cruel. He felt anger stir. He sat up and pushed her arm off his stomach.

"What's gotten into you? I'm just saying what the truth is. No white man wants to lay with a woman after she has been with an Indian. They liken it to having relations with an animal in the field, is all."

Crouching Bear stood up. He wanted to put on his garments and leave the room but he couldn't locate them. His aggression was building and the frustration of not finding his clothes added to it like tossing whiskey on a flame. His head looked around, searching the darkness for his outfit.

"You know, I could charge you for lying with me but I did this out of the kindness of my heart." Minnie put her hands on her hips. "The boys brought us your sob story and I figured I could make life a little fun for you with all your troubles. And instead you get all sore with me. You're lucky to be with a girl like me, you know."

Crouching Bear moved her aside so he could check under the bed. But he had used a little too much force and Minnie took it as the beginning of a beating. She scratched at his chest and yelled at him for being an animal. The pains overtook him immediately. He fell to the wood floor and clawed at the boards beneath his hands. His skin stretched and filled with coarse, dark hair. The bones in his spine and legs crunched as they extended and shifted into the form of a bear. Minnie sat back upon the bed, her mouth opened wide in disbelief at what she saw. She put her arm in front of her face to fend him off.

The man-bear stood eight feet tall and roared at the ceiling. It lowered its head and thrust its jaws upon Minnie. The man-bear forced its way inside her chest cavity, devouring her heart and lungs. It ate with fervor and didn't stop.

Minnie stared at the ceiling, no longer seeing. Her lifeless body thrashed upon the blood-soaked sheets as the man-bear tore hunks of flesh, its sharpened teeth mashing through meat and bone.

CHAPTER 11

"innie?" Knock, knock, knock. "Minnie? Your time is up. You have another gentleman waiting to see you." Candy waited at the door, listening for Minnie to acknowledge her. She waited for a few more seconds. "I'll see if I can keep him company for a few more minutes but you have to finish up, okay?" She leaned against the door but the noise from the lounge down the hall and the saloon downstairs was so loud she couldn't be sure if she would have heard Minnie anyway. Candy shrugged and hurried down the hall to the lounge.

The man-bear jumped up when the loud knocking sounded on the door. Its instincts for self-preservation overrode its thirst for blood. It panted quietly as it listened to the human on the other side of the door. The bear had nearly finished its meal.

Slowly, the beast's body shifted back into human form. Crouching Bear writhed silently in pain, becoming aware of the cold, hard floor boards and the overwhelming stench of death. He tried to make sense of his whereabouts but it took several minutes for his consciousness to return. He tasted blood and noticed the sticky remnants on his hands and chest.

It all came back to him, as he scrambled for his garments. He began to remember the boy's mother and their union. Then he recalled her hurtful words and his anger. His stomach churned at the thought of what he had done. This was the second time now. Crouching Bear knew the curse was real and he thought he had figured out the curse was triggered by anger. He wondered how he could possibly avoid it from happening again. Everywhere he turned there were hostile white men or his tribe hunting him down. He just couldn't imagine a time or place where he could cushion himself against the feelings of rage.

Crouching Bear found his garments wadded up beneath the sheets on the bed. Luckily, the blood, which covered most of the mattress, was concentrated toward the head of the bed. His clothes were stuffed at the foot.

As he rushed to get his clothing on, he worried about his plan to escape. The building was full of people and someone had to know he was in here with Minnie. So, even if he was lucky enough to escape, he knew he would have another hunting party on his hands. He cursed the spirits for frowning upon him. Crouching Bear picked up a yellow dress that was draped over a chair in the corner. He wiped the sticky blood from his hands and face on the dress and then tossed it under the bed.

He approached the door and gently placed his head against it, listening for activity on the other side. The noise was loud in the hallway. Crouching Bear remembered that the hallway led to the waiting lounge, where, at this hour, there would be several men and women passing the time until rooms became available. He would have to get past those people and then go down the long staircase to the saloon below, which would be filled with white men and guns. His route was filled with danger at every step.

Crouching Bear took a step back and paused to figure out how to get away. He tapped his hidden knife, sheathed inside his pant leg. It was a big knife and he kept it very sharp but he would have to fight through twenty or thirty people, at a minimum, to get out. And that's if nobody was quick enough to draw a pistol on him, which he was positive somebody would be.

Perplexed, his eyes roamed the room for other weapons when he realized there was a window on the far side of the bed. Excited, Crouching Bear crawled over Minnie's remains and peered out the glass. The window overlooked the front corner of the building. A short portion of roof tile, which hung over the front sidewalk, sat below the window.

Crouching Bear decided it was his best option. He raised the window and stuck his head out, sensing the cool, fresh night air. There were people walking in front of the building along the street. However, the side street between the saloon and the next building was dark and empty. He stretched his upper body through the window and swung his leg around. Tapping his foot quietly, he felt for the roof tile below to secure his footing. Once he was satisfied, he swung his other leg over the sill and tapped for tile again. As he did so, he looked at the bed under the window. A mosaic of blood splatter covered the bedding and the walls around it. The guilt of his actions settled in his gut and he felt remorseful for what he had done. Before the curse, his anger never would have caused him to harm a woman like that, unless he was warring and part of the warrior soul.

He rested his forehead on the window sill as he remembered his new friends. Crouching Bear worried that his killing would hurt the little boy and the town might turn against the boys for taking him in and standing up for him. He was an animal, just like they had accused in the streets.

Crouching Bear shimmied around the corner on the roof tiles, with one hand grasping the window frame. His other hand searched for anything to support his balance as he worked his way around the side of the edifice.

CHAPTER 12

C andy looked around apprehensively. She hoped Minnie would re-emerge soon. Candy liked Mr. Stapleton but she was running out of things to talk about. She felt confident she could entertain waiting guests while the girls cleaned themselves up. But that was usually for a few minutes. Minnie was pushing the limits as it had already been closer to ten minutes. Candy was grateful that Mr. Stapleton seemed to be enjoying himself in the lounge, but she feared the moment he lost interest. He might carry on and get Filler involved. Then all the girls would be getting a lecture in the morning and their pay would most likely be docked a nickel.

Mr. Stapleton kept rambling about his travels from the east coast. He paused periodically to sip his brandy and wet his whistle. Apparently he was oblivious to Candy's apprehension. He guffawed at something he had said but Candy had not really been listening. She smiled and chuckled as he patted her knee. Candy tried to maintain eye contact and re-engage herself in the conversation. But it was burdensome.

"If you'll excuse me a moment, Mr. Stapleton." She interrupted his most recent tale about a train ride through the Appalachians. "I'm going to see if Minnie is ready to receive you now." As she stood, Mr. Stapleton smacked her backside and made a lewd comment about what else a woman would be "receiving" tonight. Candy thought to herself that men were only "gentlemen" for a period before the beast showed itself. Mr. Stapleton was dressed in refined attire and spoke eloquently, but he was still just a wolf in sheep's clothing. Like all the rest, she noted.

Candy bustled through the small crowd in the lounge. She had gotten extremely frustrated with Minnie. Her job was to keep things moving in the brothel and to run interference on some matters, but Minnie had taken full advantage and she was not pleased. After all, the girls were paid much better for their services than she was for her job. Even though she preferred to have her dignity and keep her clothes on, she still believed her function was on par with the working girls.

Candy rapped her knuckles on the door with more force this time. "Minnie, time is up and you must dismiss the caller immediately. Mr. Stapleton has been more than patient with you." She waited for a response but none was forthcoming. She knocked harder this time and glanced awkwardly up the hallway to the lounge. Luckily, nobody had bothered to look in her direction or pay any attention.

Reaching her breaking point, Candy turned the knob and opened the door. What waited for her on the other side was unfathomable. She absorbed the horrific scene with wide eyes. Candy screamed as loud as she could and dropped to her knees.

The people in the lounge began to funnel down the hall to Candy's aid. Nobody knew what the screams were about until they reached the screaming woman and witnessed the blood-soaked interior of the bedroom. Word quickly spread up the hallway. As more people from the saloon reached the lounge in response to the screams, the story had already spread. Everyone in the building knew the Indian had killed Minnie.

James had returned to the saloon to fetch some water. Carson had fallen asleep minutes after they had settled in the hiding spot. Carson's deep, rhythmic breathing let James know he had plenty of time to return to town for water and to retrieve Crouching Bear before George found out the truth. James fought the restlessness as best he could but his nervous energy wouldn't allow him to relax.

When he climbed the porch to the back door of the bar, James noticed an eerie quietness emanating from inside. The usual din was subdued and the noise resembled a droning rather than an uproarious party. He paused before opening the door, leaning against the wood to listen closer. James heard what sounded like a serious conversation, marked with periodic cries. Sad cries. Women crying.

He opened the door and the saloon was only half full. Several patrons consoled a few of the ladies, who were crying into their lace handkerchiefs. The staircase to the brothel was full of people standing about, nodding their heads and talking. James sensed something was wrong and he began to approach the stairs. He was worried about his mother and he wanted to make sure she was safe.

Filler was squeezing down the stairs between the stacks of folks who lingered. He reached the bottom step at the same time James was about to climb up. Filler put his hands on James' shoulders, holding him in place. "Ya don't wanna go up there, boy. It's no place for a runt." His words were harsh but his tone signaled a warning, laced with sadness.

James immediately imagined that Filler meant his mother was harmed so he shucked off the man's hands and pushed his way up. Filler's voice followed him, getting louder and more urgent as he made his way. James tuned it out. He never made eye contact with the people he passed on the stairs. Wiggling through arms and coattails, James made his way across the lounge and down the overcrowded hall. As he reached the open door at the end of the hallway, Mr. Stapleton grabbed his elbow to anchor him before he saw the horrors inside. But James wouldn't be stopped. He shoved Mr. Stapleton and stood in the doorway to Minnie's room.

He was frozen, awestruck by the mosaic of blood splatter and the disarray of the bedding. His mother was on her knees, crying, and trying to collect bloody shreds of clothing from the floor. She saw James out of the corner of her eyes and she stopped what she was doing to rush to his side. Sarah grasped James' head and crushed it to her bosom, trying to block out the images from her boy's sight. It was too late.

James was in shock but managed to ask his mother what had happened. She caressed his hair and whispered in his ear. "It was the

Indian. He killed Minnie." James couldn't believe what she was saying. Crouching Bear was not a killer. He was quiet and intense but he would never hurt James or Carson, or their mothers. His mind fumbled to figure out how this could have happened. He realized Crouching Bear wasn't in the room.

"Where is he? Where did he go?"

Sarah looked into James' eyes. "Nobody knows. He must have gone out the window because it was open and no one saw him exit the room through the door." She searched his eyes. "Where is Carson?"

James' heart sank. He realized Carson would be devastated by the news. But he was grateful Carson was sleeping in the hiding spot and completely unaware of what had taken place tonight. "I know where he is." He took his mother's hands from his face. "I'll keep him away for awhile. And I won't tell him the news...just yet."

Sarah nodded to him as tears flowed down her cheeks. James turned and began to work his way back through the crowd. He needed to make sure Carson stayed away from town for now. He also needed to find Crouching Bear. James had to know the truth. And he wanted to get to the man before any posse was formed.

CHAPTER 13

The saloon was packed to capacity. The room was so full some people were seated on the stairs to the brothel. A cacophony of anger encircled the townsfolk as everyone fought to have their opinion heard.

Sheriff Cody Danvers scratched his dark beard as he surveyed the room. His beady eyes covered the faces in the back of the saloon and then rose up the stairs, taking personal inventory of all the attendees.

"Quiet! Quiet! Settle down, now!" Mayor Vance Cosby raised his voice to command attention. His pot belly drooped over his thick brown belt, straining to keep everything together. The mayor removed his round-rimmed glasses and fogged the lenses with his breath. Using his handkerchief, he cleaned the glasses and returned them to his round face. "I said quiet now!"

The sheriff placed his fingers inside his wrinkled cheeks and blew a piercing whistle. The crowd immediately quieted. Some voices rose again as the folks figured their opinion would now be heard but they were quickly dampened by the sheriff's menacing glare.

"Listen up. Everyone knows we are gathered here to deliberate about what needs to be done." Sheriff Danvers paused to make eye contact with the people in the room. "It is important we all remain calm and nobody goes off half-cocked."

The crowd began to stir again with various shouts rising from the back of the room. Mayor Cosby was not one to be overshadowed and he stepped up to the center of the floor. "We all know that Injun came into this town and killed poor Minnie. That Injun must account for his actions." Another round of shouting rippled through the crowd.

"Hold on, people. Let's remember what our good Lord has taught us about turning the other cheek. We must not give in to the temptation of doing the devil's work." Reverend Larson stood off to the left, with his Bible clutched firmly in hand. A bead of sweat glistened upon his furry brow. His collar constricted his chubby neck, turning his face red against his slicked back blond hair.

"How about an eye for an eye, Padre?" George threw in his two cents, as he leaned against the end of the bar. He continued to chew his tobacco, as he examined his dirty fingernails. Another roar of agreement from the angry townspeople.

The sheriff stepped forward to reclaim control of the room. "I think we all agree the Indian must be captured to stand trial for this crime. But, it will be done with an organized posse and under my command. Anyone failing to abide by my orders will be jailed for breaking the law."

"And what law is that, Sheriff?" Mayor Cosby's bushy gray mustache twitched, as he tried to override the sheriff.

Sheriff Danvers squared himself to the mayor. "My law." He held his gaze upon the mayor, who fidgeted before looking to the crowd which had gone silent. Sheriff Danvers was not a big man. In fact, he was slight by most standards but, what he lacked in size, he made up for with gun skills and aggression. The town had witnessed his "law" in action enough times to know he was not one to be tangled with.

"What about Carson?" James filled the silence with his question. The people looked from side to side to find out where the question had come from. James pushed his way through the crowd to the front of the saloon.

"What about him?" Mayor Cosby eyed James as if he were an annoyance.

"I think Carson will die if he finds out that his mother has been killed."

"Probably the most humane thing that could happen to him." The mayor mumbled under his breath.

"I don't want Carson to find out what happened to his mother. He won't be able to handle it."

The sheriff responded to James. "Where is Carson, son?"

"I got him hidden away before the news about his mother spread. He has no idea what has happened."

Reverend Larson stepped up. "What do you suggest we do, James?"

James looked down at his boots before responding. "I think we should all pretend his mom went away for a while."

"And how do we do that, young man?" Mayor Cosby furrowed his gray brows.

"I don't know. Um, we could say she left town to visit a sick relative. To, uh, take care of them and she won't be back until they are better."

"And what happens to the boy in the meantime?"

James looked the mayor in the eyes with seriousness. "I will tend to Carson like family. I mean, he practically is my little brother. And I will watch over him every day." James glanced at his mother, whose eyes were full of tears. She smiled at James with pride.

Reverend Larson placed his hand on James' shoulder. "I think the dear Lord would overlook a lie such as this. One that is filled with love and devotion. God bless you, Master James."

The crowd mumbled in agreement that everyone would protect little Carson from the truth about his mother's death. James nodded, to the folks in the room, his appreciation. He knew the news would devastate Carson and he was willing to do whatever it took to keep Carson from harm's way.

Sheriff Danvers removed his hat and ran his fingers through the curly dark hair. He nodded his head to indicate that the mayor and the pastor should fall back in with the crowd. "I will select a posse of men fit to travel with me. The deputy will be in charge of the town until I return. Anybody who opposes the deputy in my absence will answer to me personally. Understood?" The crowd nervously shuffled their feet and nobody made a sound.

"Good. Murphy, Hannigan, Jepson, Thomas. Prepare to saddle up at noon. We'll meet at the jail. Everyone else, go about your business as you would any other day. Justice will be served. You have my word on it."

Sheriff Danvers placed his hat back on his head and stepped aside as the townspeople left the saloon. The chatter was minimal, as they knew the sheriff was more than capable of backing up his words.

James remained in place as the people brushed past him. He wanted to be part of the posse too. He waited for the crowd to disperse before approaching the sheriff. As the pastor and the mayor both waddled out of the saloon, James took his chance.

"Sheriff Danvers, I want to be part of the posse."

The sheriff was the same height as James, yet the strength in his eyes made him appear much taller to James. "Ordinarily, I would box your ears and toss you out on the street. But because you graciously offered to look out for the boy I will pretend you never said anything to me." He tipped the brim of his hat and turned to leave the saloon. James grabbed the sheriff's elbow, making the man turn in anger at the transgression.

"Sheriff, I need to find Crouching Bear. I have to know what happened and why he would do such a thing to Carson's mother. I have to do it for Carson."

The sheriff yanked his elbow out of James' grasp. "Don't ever lay hands upon me again, boy. Now you go get that boy and you look after him like you said you would. I already chose the men that will assist me in bringing the Indian to justice. Real men. There ain't no room for a boy on a job like this."

James' eyes filled with tears of frustration. He knew he was man enough to handle this, even if everyone only saw him as a boy. He was determined to go, one way or the other. As Sheriff Danvers stomped out of the saloon, James wiped his eyes. He had to come up with his own plan, fast.

CHAPTER 14

James laid out his belongings on the bed. He didn't own much, but life in a small town didn't require much. Besides the clothes on his back, he had a pair of dungarees, a button-down brown cotton shirt, two pairs of underwear and two pairs of wool socks. A cowhide jacket hung off the bed post. As he took inventory of his few belongings, he began to stuff his travel sack.

Several minutes before he had gathered his things, his mother had fought him on his plan. She argued that going after Crouching Bear alone was foolish. She said he was too young and not skilled enough to protect himself against the dangers of the wild frontier. Sarah adamantly opposed his plan. James told his mother he would sneak out without her knowing if she didn't allow him to go. He told her, one way or the other, he was going. Sarah pleaded with him to stay and take care of Carson like he promised the town he would.

In James' mind, he just couldn't stay behind when he knew Crouching Bear was out there somewhere, being hunted like an animal. Crouching Bear had been his friend and he owed it to him to be the one who would bring him to justice. Plus, he had always itched to go on an adventure and this would be the perfect opportunity to prove he could handle it.

He still found it difficult to reconcile the fact that Crouching Bear had killed Minnie. While all the evidence pointed to Crouching Bear's guilt, James knew the man he had befriended could not be capable of such an act. He wanted to get the truth straight from Crouching Bear, before the town condemned the man without giving him a fair trial.

James examined his knife. He had kept it sharp since the day it was given to him by one of his mother's customers. The man was a regular and took a liking to James, who was too little to be left alone. He would play on the floor in the corner of the room, hidden behind the dressing blind while his mother worked. The man would always bring something new to James to occupy his attention. The knife was the greatest of all the things the man had given him. Sarah had protested that it was dangerous but the man insisted that all boys needed to own a knife and learn how to use one. James tested the edge of the blade, satisfied it was plenty sharp. He slid the knife back into its leather sheath and fastened it to his belt.

The bedroom door swung open without a knock. George filled the doorway in silence. James rolled his eyes knowing his mother had gotten George to threaten him against leaving. She knew he was too old to force him to stay, but she probably wanted to try a more persuasive tactic, like getting George to scare the crap out of him.

"Where you heading?"

"Look, George. I know my mother sent you here to give me a thrashing about leaving town, but I am going. And there is nothing she can do to stop me. Including sending you."

George spat tobacco juice but missed the spittoon. James didn't care because he wasn't going to be around to clean it up this time. George took two steps into the room. "You really think you can handle yourself, kid?"

"I'm not a kid anymore. And yes. I got my father's blood."

"Blood ain't gonna matter when you got Injuns attacking you or a six-shot in yer face." He scratched his stubble and leveled his blue eyes on James.

"It's my fault this happened. I have to go." James slumped down on the bed. For the first time since the meeting, he showed his vulnerability. "I brought Crouching Bear into the bar and introduced him to my mother and Minnie. And so, if anyone deserves to go out into the dangerous wild to fetch him, it ought to be me." He sighed out loud.

George looked him over. His dusty leather jacket and chaps creaked as he rested his hands on his gun belt. "Well, you definitely made a big mistake bringing a wild man into the saloon. Big mistake." He took another two steps toward James. "But you'll be making a bigger mistake if you go out on your own. You need backup."

James raised his head. He wasn't sure but it sounded as if George was agreeing with his plan to go after Crouching Bear. "What?"

"Maybe a man like you needs a man like me to ride with." George wasn't smiling but the tone of his voice suggested a smile was behind the words.

"Are you serious? But what about your job? And my mom? And what about Sheriff Danvers?"

George scratched his stubble and looked down at his boots. "Well, I reckon Filler don't really need me on account of him being able to handle himself. And your mother asked me to watch over you once she realized you were going to go no matter what she said." He looked back at James. "And I don't like Danvers so I don't much care for what he thinks."

James jumped off the bed and ran over to George. He hugged the large man as tight as he could and then stepped back. George made a face that showed his discomfort. James noticed and apologized for his excited gesture. "I thought you didn't like me."

"I don't. But I want to get that Injun that killed Minnie. And I respect your momma for how she has always treated me like a person, unlike every other turd in this town." He pushed James back a step. "So let's get something clear. I don't like you. At all. And there will not be any more touching me of any sort. I'm doing this for revenge and for your momma. Nothing else." George thought about it a second. "Well, maybe to anger Danvers and Filler, too."

James clapped his hands together. He was excited he was finally going on an adventure, even though it was for a bad reason. He snatched up his sack and spun around to get started. When he turned, George's outstretched hand contained a silver pistol with a worn wooden handle. He held it by the barrel with the handle toward James. James' eyes opened wide as he admired the pistol. "You'll be needing one of these once we get outside of town." He handed James the gun. James turned the pistol over in his hands as he admired every square inch of it. As he spun it around, the barrel pointed at George. "Don't. Point it. At me."

James realized he wasn't holding a toy and began to handle it more carefully. He tucked the pistol inside his belt loop, against his back, so he could hide it under his jacket. He was floating in the clouds now that he was a man with a gun going on an adventure. As soon as he realized the serious nature of his travels, he got more serious. "Okay. Before we go, I have one more thing to do."

CHAPTER 15

"Where'd she go?"

James took a deep breath before replying to Carson. "Well, she got a telegram that one of her relatives was real sick and needed her help. So she packed up and took the first coach out of town." He helped Carson climb out of the hiding spot.

"Which relative?"

"I'm not sure." He started to sweat because Carson was making him work hard on this lie. "She didn't have time to say. She just said she would be gone for a while and that I was to look after you." James knocked a burr off Carson's sleeve.

"Can I sent her a letter?" Carson blinked incessantly with the sun in his eyes.

"It's send, not sent. Uh, I guess so. We can write her a letter, in a few days, when I get back to town." James ruffled Carson's hair.

"Where are you going, James?"

"I, uh, have to go see if I can find Crouching Bear. He's, um, lost." James kicked at the dirt to avoid eye contact with Carson, who seemed to look right through him.

"I wanna go too. He's my friend and I don't want him lost."

James cursed himself under his breath. He loved Carson like a brother but this kid was making things so difficult. "It's just that, um, where Crouching Bear is lost might be real dangerous. And I don't want you to get hurt."

"But, if it is dangerous, won't you get hurt too?"

James looked to the blue skies for answers. He thought, to himself, he really should have spent more time preparing for this conversation. He figured it would be relatively easy since Carson was slow. Suddenly, Carson was a schoolhouse graduate. "Nah, it isn't too dangerous for adults, just kids. You know, lots of Indians and big animals and junk. But I'll be okay." He knew his reasoning was lame but he hoped it did the trick. "George will be coming with me as protection."

"George doesn't like you though."

James smiled at Carson. He sometimes realized Carson was sharper than people gave him credit for being. He knew that firsthand, as Carson whipped him every time they played cards. "No, he doesn't like me very much. But he promised to look after me while we search for Crouching Bear."

"But I will be lonely without you and my momma. Who will play cards with me?" Carson moped with his chin on his chest.

"My mother will play cards with you. And she will help you handle my chores while I am gone. So you will have plenty to keep you busy." James tossed in the chores concept at the last second.

"Oh boy. You mean, Mister Filler will let me sweep the floor and wipe the tables and squeeze the wet rags on the porch?" For the first time this morning, Carson looked happy. James nodded and looked off in the distance. He found it harder to keep up the lie with each successive answer. He knew it was all for Carson's own good to keep him in the dark about the true nature behind the travel. Or was it? Was it just more important that he go off on an adventure than live up to his responsibilities? Responsibilities he undertook willingly and publicly? James tried not to think too deeply about it, afraid he wouldn't like the answer he arrived at.

"You understand I will always protect you, right?"

"Sure, James. You are my brother from a different mother like my momma says." Carson smiled up at James with one eye closed to avoid the sun. He punched James in the shoulder.

James' eyes watered as he thought about how much Carson meant to him. He really was like his little brother and he loved Carson so much. "Yup, brothers from a different mother." James repeated, trying not to remember the horrific image of Minnie torn apart.

CHAPTER 16

C rouching Bear scanned the blue sky for answers. The warmth of the sun dried the last tears that wet his cheeks. A mild breeze from the west blew his long black hair across his face. The tall, dry weeds tickled his bottom as they danced in the wind. The smell of his bowel movement disgusted him as it was putrid with human remains.

He tried to shift his thoughts from the previous night toward his survival but it was no use. Each time he thought of where to hide or how he was going to eat, it reminded him of why he was now in this predicament.

Crouching Bear felt horrible for what he had done to Minnie. More importantly, he felt that he had betrayed James and Carson. After all, they were the first whites to treat him well and they were really the only people who accepted him for who he was. Without conditions. Even his tribesmen only accepted him for his fighting skills and bravery. None of the tribe ever spoke to him about their dreams or their thoughts. It was all about fighting and loyalty to the tribe.

As he finished cleaning up, Crouching Bear wondered what James and Carson were doing. He figured that Carson was devastated that his mother was killed, and by one of his very own friends. Crouching Bear knew that Carson was a special child by the way he saw the world. He had encountered a similar child in his tribe when he was a youth. But the child was sacrificed in order to benefit the tribe. The elders knew the child would be another mouth to feed without providing skills like hunting or fighting. So the elders convinced the child's parents to allow the sacrifice in order to appease the spirits for a bountiful hunting season. It was tragic but necessary in the small tribe.

He imagined Carson crying, failing to understand the loss of his mother. And then he pictured James consoling the youngster. Crouching Bear knew James would do whatever it took to look out for the young boy. He could see the brotherly love James had for Carson. How he always stood close to him and how he would put his arm around the boy's small shoulders. James was always careful to speak to Carson as if he was normal rather than treating him as a lesser human being. He winced at the thought of betraying James' trust. He lowered his head and squeezed his eyes closed for a moment to blot out the hurt he felt in his gut.

Crouching Bear looked east toward the town. He had traveled far enough that the town was no longer in sight. But he still worried about the posse he knew would come after him. He was a wanted man twice over now. It would be a race to see which group of hunters would find him first. The tribe or the white men?

He tried to think of the best plan of escape. The town was east and his tribe would be coming from the northeast. It would be natural to run further west or south to put distance between himself and the parties. Yet, part of him thought he might be wiser to double back a bit to the north. The hunters would probably follow the reasoning of his trail southwest. So doubling back to the north would be opposite of what they would expect him to do. However, it would bring him closer to danger. He carefully considered his options as he scanned the horizon for signs of travelers.

The loneliness began to settle inside him. He had gotten a second chance at life and it was gone as quickly as it had arrived. The images of Carson and James flashed in his mind. He had found two friends when it seemed as if the whole world had cast him out. And then he had blown it. He was doomed to roam the earth alone, forever. Cursed. He could never be with people again, even people he cared for, because he might eventually get mad and kill them. And, if he didn't kill the people he cared for, he might harm others, putting his loved ones' safety in jeopardy. His thoughts explored suicide for a brief moment but then vanished. Suicide would only damn his soul to wander the earth for eternity, thus extending his curse beyond the physical world.

Crouching Bear started to run through the tall, amber weeds. He had to keep moving, with constant vigilance, if he were to survive this plight. His shadow followed along in the afternoon sun. The running made him feel free and alive, out here on the vast plains. Flat lands all around and a wide open sky above gave him hope that the walls could only close in on him within his mind. His renewed sense of freedom spurred him on faster now. He felt the wind in his hair, as the tall weeds brushed against his legs. He closed his eyes while he ran, feeling the earth unfold beneath his feet. His mind reached out to the heavens as if he were a soaring eagle. He opened his eyes and continued to run as fast as he could. For a moment, Crouching Bear smiled.

CHAPTER 17

J ames had butterflies in his stomach. He and George had been
traveling for a little over an hour now but his nervousness had still
not subsided. The sheer excitement of going on an adventure like he
had always dreamed about had worn off pretty quickly. The realization
of the nature of the adventure had slammed home and settled deep in
his gut. This adventure wasn't going to be fun after all. He had to hunt
down his new friend, Crouching Bear. And he had left behind his mother
and his best friend for the first time in his life. James had never
experienced a longing for home and family before now. He didn't really
like how it felt.

George rode alongside James quietly. James knew George was a
man of few words but he realized this was going to be a long, lonely trip.
He looked over at the large man who appeared monstrous on top of his
dark horse. George felt James' eyes upon him and returned his gaze. He
spat a juicy plume of tobacco between the horses and then turned his
head forward. James sighed to himself that at least he wouldn't have to
clean up George's mess out here.

James had argued with George as they prepped the horses. George
wanted to put an all-time beating on Crouching Bear and then drag him

back to town, literally. James preferred a more subtle approach of tracking down his Indian friend and asking him what had happened. He still didn't think that Crouching Bear would just do something so randomly violent. But he figured, if he did, there had to be a real good reason for it. After James got his answer, he intended to bind Crouching Bear's hands and ride with him back into town to answer to the charges. The thought of a trial caused James concern as he knew there would be no way to hide the truth from Carson at that point. A pang of sorrow for his little buddy rumbled through his chest.

George stopped his horse and James followed suit. The large man lifted his hat off his sweaty forehead and took a swig from his canteen. James' stomach took an extra turn when he realized George drank the water and swallowed it while the tobacco was still lumped in his cheek. George squinted at the sun above and then pointed to the ground a few feet behind them.

"That there is an Injun mark." James grimaced with confusion and asked what George meant. "Yer red pal was here by the looks of that print. Animals leave prints with claws. Boots leave a toe and heal print. Injuns leave a flat, elongated print like that on account of their moccasins." He reset the brim of his hat to shadow his eyes from the sun.

James thought to himself how glad he was that George had come along with him. Even though he didn't particularly like George, he knew skills like this were going to be critical. And they were skills James didn't have. He wasn't searching the ground for indications at all. James thought following the line of the horizon for movement or puffs of smoke would lead him to Crouching Bear. But it was quickly becoming apparent that finding the man was going to be much more difficult than he had originally imagined.

"Well, at least we appear to be headed in the right direction."

"It ain't by chance that we came across that print, kid. I've been scouting signs since we left town. Yer red pal is good about keeping to grassy land but, when we hit these dried out patches, there ain't no hiding." George leaned over the horn of the saddle and rubbed his horse's neck. "He's got a head start on us but we'll catch up if we play it right." George spat and wiped the dark juice from his stubble with the sleeve of his jacket. "And when we do, I'm gonna wring his red neck."

"Nobody is going to touch him, George." James' anger spiked before he could check his words. "I mean, we are supposed to bring him back to town for trial. So we can't hurt him without cause. I don't want to talk about this again." James shifted his eyes away from George when he sensed George's agitation.

"How can you live with yerself knowing what that savage did to Minnie? He just waltzed into town and took advantage of our hospitality like that and you are ready to fergive him for it?" George glared at James.

"Look, we don't know all the facts is all I'm saying. Crouching Bear will answer for it but not at our hands. It ain't right."

"Was it right fer him to tear her up like that and leave that dumb boy an orphan?"

"Don't call Carson dumb. He ain't dumb, he is just different." James spun in his saddle and faced the large man head on. "I am the one bringing Crouching Bear in. You are here to help me and watch over me. But I am the one making the decisions. It's my call." James maintained his glare without flinching. He felt the hair on his neck rise with his blood pressure. His skin began to warm, from the inside out, with the surge of adrenaline.

George spat again, this time striking James' horse's rump. The darkened juice dripped from the light brown skin of the horse. He sat up in his saddle and tugged on the reins while spurring the stirrup. He trotted forward without a word. James sighed to himself. He was afraid of George and knew the big man would whoop him something fierce. But his frustration got the better of him and he had challenged George directly. James wondered how many men actually got away with such an incident with George. He figured probably none.

As his anger deflated, he tugged on the reins and tried to catch up with George. The journey would be difficult enough without the two men fighting. James thought he should apologize to George for his hostility. Would George take an apology as a sign of weakness? Was it better to stand up to a man as a strong man should? What did he really have to apologize for anyway? George was out of line for wanting to take justice into his own hands, especially with Crouching Bear, who deserved a chance to explain his actions. James struggled with how he should handle all this new territory he was traversing. As an adult. For the first time. He knew this journey was as much an emotional and mental journey as it was a physical one of riding across the plains.

James rode on as he wondered what he had gotten himself into.

CHAPTER 18

J ames and George crested a sloping hilltop and surveyed the valley below. A grove of hack-berry trees offset the flat expanse. A thin wisp of smoke rose from within the shaded confines, quickly dispersing in the wind. Only a trained eye would pick up the plume. George saw it right away.

James noticed George studying the grove below. George nodded at it and they both spurred their horses to approach slowly. A hundred yards from the trees, they dismounted their horses and continued the rest of the way on foot. George freed his rifle from the saddle pouch, while James withdrew the pistol from the belt loop of his dungarees.

Inside the shady stand of trees, a small fire burned. A stick spit held a small muskrat carcass, which was blackened on the bottom but nearly raw on top. There was no sign of anyone. James stuffed his pistol back under his belt and walked straight to the fire. As he walked, he saw George roll his eyes at him from behind a tree. Before James could react to his own carelessness, he felt a long knife blade press against his throat.

"Come on out from behind that tree." James heard the man behind him speak to George. He saw George step halfway out from his cover. He spat tobacco juice without wiping up the drops that collected on his chin. George's eyes narrowed, making it difficult to see what he was focusing on.

"Come now. What brings you to my home?"

"Take it easy, old man. We're just looking for an Injun that done something wrong. We ain't got no beef with you. Unless you want one."

James was surprised George referred to the man behind him as old. James hadn't yet laid eyes on him, but, from the strength in his hands, old was the last thing James would have imagined.

"Injun, huh? What makes you think there's an Injun in this patch of woods?"

George held his hands out in front of him to show he meant no harm. However, the rifle was still in his right hand. "That's what we were checking on when we came in here. A man don't know nothing until he knows something."

The man holding the knife to James' throat laughed. He let go of James. "Sounds about right."

James turned and saw a short, old man with long gray hair. The man slid his knife back in its sheath and extended his arm toward the fire. James didn't know what to make of it so he waited to see what George would do. George lowered his arms and slowly approached the fire.

"I don't have much but you are welcome to a little lunch before you continue looking for your Injun." The old man flipped his long hair back and sat on the grass next to the fire.

George set his gun down as he plopped to the grass. James followed George's lead. They looked at each other and then back at the old man. George nodded at the old man. James spoke first. "Thank you, sir."

The old man handed James and George carrots that still had soil on them. James brushed his carrot on his pant leg. George bit into his carrot, soil and all. James realized George still had a wad of tobacco in his cheek. He couldn't believe the man could eat food with that stuff in his mouth.

"So, let's hear about this Injun and what he did that has you out here looking for him."

James glanced at George who was busy chewing his carrot. "Well, sir..."

"Please. My name is Soaring Eagle."

George stopped chewing; one cheek lumped out with carrot, the other with tobacco. James was speechless. Here they were searching for

Crouching Bear and George kept referring to him in the slang. But now they were talking to another Indian. James was confused because this man did not look like an Indian. He had the long hair, sure, but many wilderness men grew out their hair. This man had fairer skin than all the Indians James had ever seen. Admittedly, he hadn't seen any other than Crouching Bear.

"Uh, sorry, Mr. Eagle, I mean…oh boy." James was flustered.

Soaring Eagle leaned back and laughed hard as he removed the meat from the skewer. He seemed to take great delight in James' awkwardness. He broke off a rear leg and handed it to James as his laughter subsided. He tossed the other back leg across the flames to George. He tore a slice of charred meat from the side of the carcass with his dirty fingernails and slurped it up.

"You're an Indian?" James tried to recover. He looked at Soaring Eagle under raised eyebrows.

"A man has to do what he can to survive these days. I dress to blend in." Soaring Eagle indicated his white man clothing.

"A wolf in sheep's clothing." George condemned the man with his tone as much as his words.

"Perhaps to some it would appear that way. However, this wolf doesn't eat sheep." Soaring Eagle grinned wide, as he tried to set his guests at ease.

George snorted under his breath and continued gnawing on the leg bone; his eyes watching Soaring Eagle closely.

James wanted to reset the conversation so he related the tale of Crouching Bear coming to town after being ostracized by his own tribe, how he and Carson saved him from trouble and then the final act which set them on this course to find the fugitive. The whole time James spoke he noticed Soaring Eagle listening with great interest. Soaring Eagle nodded with understanding throughout the story.

"Finding a dangerous man like that can be very difficult."

"We are expert trackers. We've followed his markers so far." George tossed the leg bone into the fire, sucking the juice off his greasy fingers.

"Hm. Tracking and finding are two different things, no?" Soaring Eagle spoke with an air of wisdom that James admired. He wished he was as sure about the ways of the world as this old man seemed to be. "I might be able to help you fellas in such matters."

James waited for more but Soaring Eagle paused. James glanced at George, who was still studying the old man closely. His eyes shifted to James momentarily and then back to the old man.

"In my world, the tribe relies on an expert to shepherd folks to the truths as they are written in the sky. The spirits reveal these truths to those who know how to read them. I am such an expert."

James and George exchanged glances. Soaring Eagle smiled and offered another portion of muskrat.

CHAPTER 19

The darkness within the hack-berry grove was palpable. Soaring Eagle had shielded the fire by enclosing it within a screen of animal skins, adding to the darkness. He said it would prevent the glow of the flames from attracting unwanted visitors. The old man handed James a concoction he had just brewed.

"What's in it?" James accepted the earthenware cup.

"A little of this and a little of that."

George protested immediately. "We ain't drinking nothing we don't understand, old man."

Soaring Eagle ignored George. "Ancient peoples in these lands have traveled with the spirit guides many times. I assure you, the tea is not harmful."

James sniffed the brew and recoiled from its strong aroma. It smelled like something from an outhouse and he was not very keen about having it pass his lips. "Ugh, it smells horrible."

Soaring Eagle laughed. "It smells powerful because it requires much to reach the heavens. You must drink it down and then lie back to fly with the spirits."

"And once I drink this, I will find Crouching Bear through my dreams?"

Soaring Eagle nodded.

James thought about all his dreams of adventure, but never in his life had he envisioned an adventure like this. He was on the precipice of trusting a strange old man, an Indian man no less. And drinking a foul-smelling liquid so he could have magical dreams. It sounded crazy in his head. He couldn't help wondering if his father had ever done something as wild as this. James shrugged and then nodded at George.

"I'll make sure you're safe. If anything happens to you, I will wear this old man's skin for pajamas." George pointed at Soaring Eagle with his bowie knife.

Soaring Eagle kept smiling. "Fair enough. Now, let's get on with it." He indicated with his hands that James should lift the cup to his mouth.

James sniffed the brew one more time and winced at the aroma. He looked up at the stars that peeked through the small canopy of branches above. He lifted the cup to his lips and swallowed the broth down quickly. He gagged and dropped the cup to the dirt. George sat up straight in anticipation of attacking Soaring Eagle. But James recovered and nodded reassuringly at George. He burped and then lay back upon his pack. The heat, of the liquid, spread from his stomach to his extremities. A tingling sensation grew in his fingertips and he closed his eyes.

Within seconds, James was gone. His body was no longer anchored to the earth. The night breeze carried him gently across the sky. He felt weightless and thought this must be what it felt like to be an angel. James no longer heard Soaring Eagle or George. The smell of the fire was replaced with the freshness of a spring morning. He knew he floated high above the ground, even though blackness surrounded him.

The sensations of floating and freedom from earthbound limitations consumed James. He smiled to himself in sheer ecstasy at this novel experience. It did feel magical and he sort of hoped he would remain in this state forever. It was peaceful and exciting. His body drifted along the currents of air, circling in increasingly smaller loops until he approached a wooded lot. As his dream-being landed gently in a thick patch of pine needles, James saw Crouching Bear. The man was nestled under a pile of leaves with his knees pulled up to his chest. The smell of decaying brush filled James' nostrils. Crouching Bear sat up, startled. His knife at the ready, the Indian strained to see through the darkness. James tried to jump back from a potential assault but he had no control of his body. He just stood still in the pine needles, watching Crouching Bear. He tried to speak with him but words would not come out. Apparently, the spirits brought James to this place but he was unable to interact as he would in the physical world.

Crouching Bear sniffed the air and looked around with nervousness. James could tell by his reaction that Crouching Bear sensed his presence. But he must be invisible. He giggled to himself as it reminded him of playing hide and seek with Carson. James caught his breath, as it seemed he and Crouching Bear had locked eyes. His heart skipped a beat. Deep inside Crouching Bear's gaze, James thought he saw sorrow behind the fear. It felt like James was reading his true self, knowing Crouching Bear felt terrible about the tragedy that had taken place. James felt sorry for Crouching Bear, and, as he did, his body flew up into the sky. A pit filled James' stomach. He strained against the forces that carried him away, wanting to return to Crouching Bear. James had never felt such a strong connection, a link, with anyone before. Not his mother. Not even Carson. It was a bond of kindred, of knowing, of oneness.

Immediately, James' heart sank and he drifted across the sky at incredible speeds. The wonder and enjoyment had passed and was quickly replaced with pain and terror. What had seemed magical just moments ago was now a death spiral. James didn't trust this feeling anymore. He was overwhelmed with a foreboding sense of doom and tragedy. James imagined himself dying.

George sprung over the fire and landed on Soaring Eagle, his knife upon the old man's throat. "Save him. Save him right now." Tobacco juice drooled from his mouth as he spoke.

"He is fine. The body goes through several changes in order to reach out across the universe. It is normal."

George kept the knife tight against Soaring Eagle's neck. He stole a glance at James' body, writhing in a fit upon the ground. The tortured spasms had scared George. Pained expressions flashed across the boy's face and it appeared to George that the devil himself had overtaken his companion. George had never witnessed anything like it before. He kneed Soaring Eagle in the balls and rolled off the old man. Soaring Eagle shrunk into a fetal position to combat the anguish. George crawled over to James and hovered over him. He searched the expressions on the boy's face, trying to figure out what must be going on inside to create such horrific movements. George put his hand on James' chest and felt his heart thundering beneath his fingers. He glanced over at the old man, who was busy rubbing his groin and moaning. George sat back in the dirt and kept his hand on James, waiting for him to return.

James shot up like a lightning bolt had surged through his spine. George fell over from the fright of the sudden motion. James turned his head to look at George and then vomited all over the large man. His chest heaved as he struggled to catch his breath.

Soaring Eagle rolled over with a grimace of pain on his face. George stared down at his lap with his hands held high in the air. His expression revealed his disgust and surprise at his soiled garments.

James blinked a few times and then burped. "That's one mess I am not going to clean up."

Soaring Eagle laughed out loud and rolled back over in the dirt. James shrugged at George. And George just stared, incredulously, at James.

CHAPTER 20

Crouching Bear snored gently. It had been the first time, in several days, he had relaxed enough to catch up on sleep. He had scooped up a pile of rotting leaves and covered his body with them for warmth. The pine needles underneath the tree provided a soft cushion against the rocks and roots below. He thought it was going to be a long night since he couldn't light a fire to keep himself warm. He didn't want to reveal his location to his pursuers.

An urge for survival overtook his body. He sat up alertly, unsheathing his knife for protection. He was fast asleep when he felt like somebody was upon him. He squinted against the darkness to find movement. But he found nothing. He sniffed the air to pick up the scent of the intruder but again found nothing. Crouching Bear's nose was as skilled as his fighting abilities. Years of warrior training and fighting had taught his nose to pick up various scents. He could easily distinguish fear from surprise, rage from anger and other subtleties. His senses were that strong.

Crouching Bear shifted his legs without a sound. He got them ready to spring into action, to either flee or strike forward. He wasn't sure yet which way to go but at least he had readied himself for action.

The feeling of being watched went through him like a chill. He knew somebody was there, and yet they weren't. He continued to scan back and forth for movement or sound. His breath paused to sharpen his hearing.

A vision of James ran through Crouching Bear's mind. It seemed as if James were inside him, probing for answers, questioning. He tried to brush it aside and focus on his survival but failed to avoid it. The feeling of James' presence began to consume him. He felt the boy through the darkness. He thought he felt James talking to him. But there were no words. It was just a sensation he couldn't explain.

As fast as the feeling shook him from his rest, it was gone. Crouching Bear sat back against the earth, relieving the taut muscles in his legs. He felt safe again. Undisturbed.

Crouching Bear knew it was James that came to him. He also knew what it was. James had embarked on a vision quest to find him. But how? James was not versed in the ways of the spirits. At least, he didn't think he was. How could a seventeen year-old white man know how to reach Crouching Bear across the universe? It was impossible. Unless somebody had helped him. But who? James would have had to leave his town and found a shaman capable and willing to bring him into the mystical realm of the ancients. It seemed unlikely but there could be no other explanation.

Crouching Bear rubbed the sleep from his eyes. He yawned and realized another sleepless night was ahead of him. His mind twisted with thoughts of the experience. If it was truly a vision quest James had come to him through, then running would be useless. Crouching Bear knew the power of the vision quest and how it would lead James directly to him. Whether he stayed put in this spot or traveled another hundred miles, James would know how to find him.

With that thought, Crouching Bear realized the truth. James was coming for him. Why James? He expected his tribesman to hunt him down. And he knew a posse from the town would be formed to chase him. But James? James? Was James coming to kill him like everyone else? Or was he going to try to protect Crouching Bear from the other hunting parties? As much as he hoped James was coming to his aid, he couldn't help but believe his doom would be at the hands of his last true friend. What made matters worse was the fact that he felt so terrible for what he did to Carson and James. He didn't think he had the stamina to fight James off. If James was coming to kill him for his deeds, he knew he would submit completely to the will of the spirits. He deserved the punishment for what he had done to Minnie. Crouching Bear had never felt sorrier for anything in his life than the pain he had brought to Carson and James by hurting Minnie.

He slammed his fist against his thigh. It frustrated him that this curse had caused him to lose his second chance at belonging. At life. He wished he had the courage to defy the spirits and commit himself to his own death. But the eternal unrest was too much to bear, even for his sins.

The darkness closed in around him as he scanned his surroundings again. He lay down without bothering to scoop the leaves back into place. He knew he wasn't going to sleep so there would be no need of a blanket. He curled up and held his legs to his chest, thinking about the events of the last few days. It had been such a brief amount of time and such a fall from grace. The notion of a tragic tribe story being told for generations flashed within his mind. His tale would become an instructional lesson for many years. "This is what happened to the once mighty, Crouching Bear." "Don't do this or you will end up like Crouching Bear." "It could be worse; you could be frowned upon by the spirits like Crouching Bear." A tear traced his cheek and settled in his long, dark hair. He squeezed his eyes shut, forcing the rest of the tears to fall. Crouching Bear sighed to himself. He knew what he had to do. As painful as it would be, a peace found his soul, blanketing the torment that lived inside. The future had been written. He must do the bidding of the ancients. The spirits would guide him. What once was would now be done.

CHAPTER 21

James opened his eyes. The sun had risen and he squinted against the brightness. Soaring Eagle stirred an orange paste in a bowl, using the handle of his knife. George stood on the edge of the hack-berry grove, his back to James and Soaring Eagle. James wondered what George was looking at. Then he realized what he was doing, as George reached down and shook off the last few drops of morning urination. He tasted the vile flavor of his tongue, reminding him of the evil brew from last night.

"How do you feel?" Soaring Eagle asked James, without diverting his attention from stirring.

"Like I've been dragged for miles by a thousand horses."

Soaring Eagle laughed from his belly. James shot him a dirty look for finding humor at his expense. James thought to himself that the man's Indian name would be more appropriate if it were Laughing Ass. This made him smile to himself.

George entered the fire ring with his thumbs hooked in his gun belt. James nodded a good morning and George returned the nod with a juicy splat of tobacco. James shook his head. He guessed everything was the same as it ever was. He stood on wobbly legs and tried to re-orient his equilibrium. Some lingering effects from the previous night, he surmised.

Soaring Eagle stood and approached James with the bowl of orange paste. He wrinkled his nose at the thought of ingesting any more homemade recipes. "I'm not hungry, but thanks."

"This is not for eating. It is for protecting." The old man dipped two fingers in the paste and drew two lines under each of James' eyes. The vertical stripes were thick and James could smell the paste. It definitely smelled like an outhouse. "The spirits know the mark of the traveler, and walk with him. You will be protected now that you wear the mark."

George spat into the fire and a hiss sounded. "Protected from what?"

Soaring Eagle turned to face George but continued addressing James. George got the message the old man was purposely being rude to him. He shifted on his feet and rubbed his dark stubble. "Protection from the curse of the tribe which not only weighs down the cursed, but also those who come in contact with the cursed."

James wished the awful smell would go away. He raised a hand to touch the marks and then thought better of it. He didn't want that stink to be on his hands too. "Well, thanks for taking us in. And thank you for helping us find our friend, Crouching Bear."

"Not a friend." George spun and began securing his rifle and bag to the saddle.

James shrugged and smiled at Soaring Eagle. "Anyway, I appreciate your help, Soaring Eagle." He looked at his boots and then back at the old man. "It's funny. All my life I've been told that Indians are no good and they are dangerous. But the first two Indians I met were nice people."

Soaring Eagle grinned. He placed a hand on James' shoulder. "A secret." He indicated that James should lean closer to hear his whisper. James leaned forward. The old man pressed his lips against James' ear. "White man speaks out of both sides of his mouth." He slapped James' shoulder and started to laugh again. James didn't know how to respond. He just watched the old man laugh, while walking away. Then he chuckled to himself. He didn't get it but the old man's laugh was infectious.

James climbed up on his horse and situated the reins. The old man sat back down and watched as they prepared to ride off. James turned the horse toward Soaring Eagle. "How will I know? How will I find him?"

The old man squinted in the sunlight. "You won't. But the spirits will." He closed his eyes and tilted his face to the sun. "They will take you to him."

James was still confused. He didn't understand all the riddles and double talk. He resigned himself to figuring it out on his own, knowing he wouldn't get a straight answer from Soaring Eagle. He clucked his tongue and his horse turned to follow George, who was already trotting ahead. He looked back over his shoulder at the old man and gave him a timid wave.

Soaring Eagle nodded at James. The old man bent to add kindling to the fire. "And he knows you are coming." He said the words softly to himself.

James felt sick to his stomach. The wild ride he had last night still left him jittery. It was more than just the sick he let loose on George's clothes. George forgave him after calling him many cuss words James had never heard before. He didn't know they were cuss words for sure, but the tone and the sound of the words seemed like cuss words. James had heard some colorful language through the door of the saloon but nothing like the ones George used.

The bouncing of the galloping horse inflamed his upset stomach. They had just begun riding and he was already looking forward to stopping. James started to think that adventures weren't all they were cracked up to be. Long hours in the saddle. Dust and sun. Little water and food. What was supposed to be so exciting, fighting evil and running off bad guys, was missing from this campaign. He swallowed a buildup of bile in his throat.

James caught up to George, who spat in his direction rather than look at him. James wondered if he was still sore at the vomiting. George tugged the reins of his dark horse. James stopped alongside his companion.

"All right?"

"Yeah, I'm fine."

"You fixing to tell us which way we're headed?"

"Yes. I mean, no. Well, I guess so." James saw George's expression match his own confusion. "He said the spirits would lead us to him. Except they ain't said anything to me yet."

George cussed again, but this time under his breath. He tilted his brim lower to shield his eyes from the sun. "Burning daylight so I hope these spirits got lanterns." George spurred his animal and continued on, leaving James behind.

James scratched his head and wondered if he should have stayed in town. Or, at the very least, left town on his own. George's ill humor was easier to live with when he could just go upstairs or outside to avoid it. Instead, he was stuck with the big brute. Then he brightened as he recalled Carson's cheery voice in his head. He missed the little guy and knew the faster he got moving the quicker he could get back to Carson.

"Back to square one." He said the words aloud and his spirit picked up. He spurred his horse and sped up to catch George.

CHAPTER 22

Crouching Bear surveyed the horizon from the tree top. From this height, he could see for miles around. He was hidden within the dense foliage of the pines. Far to the east, he could make out a dust cloud of travelers. Judging by the lack of stealth, he assumed they were the posse from the town. White man rode in large groups for protection. And they weren't especially aware of the noise they made, nor the signs they left behind. He shook his head at how stupid white man was.

He estimated, by the distance, he had about a day to a day and a half lead on the posse. As long as he kept moving, he could stay outside their reach. But he would help them out since he had decided to follow his plan of doubling back toward the northeast. As long as he remained careful, he could pass them by in the night and they would never know he had changed direction.

His larger worry had to do with his tribesmen. They were cunning warriors, trained in the warrior spirit. They would know how to track his movements far better than the white man. And he would have to cover his tracks with much more care. These warriors were skilled at tracking and identifying tricks to cover trails. He knew the Indians would be formidable opponents.

Crouching Bear looked north to check for signs of the warriors. No signs were visible but he couldn't be sure if that was due to their stealth or the fact that they may have given up chase. If they had, the delay would only be temporary. Retribution would be too great a motivation. And so would elevated tribe status. He started back down the tree slowly, taking care to ensure his footing.

What troubled him more was facing James. He was certain now it was James' spirit which had visited him last night. Somehow James had figured out how to vision quest. And Crouching Bear knew it would only be a matter of time before they crossed paths.

He struggled with seeing James after what he had done to Minnie. His guilt overwhelmed him and it would be evident to James. He was ashamed of his betrayal. He had really grown to like James, and Carson, in such a short period of time. And to cause his caring, innocent friends such pain was inexcusable. It would be difficult to look James in the eyes and explain his actions.

Crouching Bear reached the trunk of the tree. He hopped gently down to the earth and gathered his few belongings. His stomach growled with hunger. Eating had not been much of a priority between all the running and his desire not to cook game with a fire that could be seen or smelled from a distance.

His mind shifted back to James and their inevitable rendezvous. He didn't think James would be capable of taking justice into his own hands. The boy was too innocent to kill a man, even though he was white. And he suspected the bond they had shared, before he had ruined it, was strong enough to temper James' anger. But what if James did try to execute him. Earlier, he thought he would drop to his knees and accept the death sentence should James choose to carry it out. As the hours ticked by, Crouching Bear's survival instincts began taking over. He had fleeting thoughts of how to expediently take James out in order to live on. It was an internal battle he couldn't yet come to grips with. How could he possibly hurt James more than he already had? Yet his soul wasn't quite ready to give in. He knew running from James would only delay what must come to pass. It would be better to meet it head on and get past it, or die trying.

He slung his pouch over his shoulder and took off running. As he exited the pine trees, he lowered his shoulders and bent his legs to keep his running form lower to the ground. He was outside the range of sight of his pursuers but there was no need to tempt fate. Heading northeast, Crouching Bear continued on his journey.

The posse galloped at a slower pace than Sheriff Cody Danvers liked. But this pursuit was more difficult than most others. He had hunted down his fair share of fugitives, over the years, as a lawman. But an Indian? This one was different. He understood some facets of Indian culture from his own migration west after the Civil War. Indians were downright savages. And cunning. They had survived in the wild against other warring tribes and against the spread of the white man. Not to mention the raw elements of nature. Sheriff Danvers knew this chase would be like no other.

He wanted the posse to spread out and go slowly in order to pick up the Indian's trail. He knew the Indian would be wise enough to cover his tracks or at least find ways to mix them in with game animals or travel parties in order to hide in plain sight. He also knew the Indian was on foot, not horseback. So, in Sheriff Danver's mind, going slowly should not set them too far behind as they could cover more ground in a day than the fugitive could. They would also have to stop less frequently for rest than a man traveling on his own two feet.

The sheriff glanced to his left as Murphy and Hannigan covered the southern flank. Murphy's shocking red hair and Hannigan's twisted nose stood out on their profiles. Danvers had never ridden with these boys before but he wanted them on his team this time because of their ruggedness. He had locked each of them up several times, to give them time to cool off their drunken Irish tempers, after a long night at the saloon. They were both fierce fighters and good men, even though they had a taste for booze. Out in the wild, Danvers would have their sober ferocity at his disposal.

To his right, covering the northern flank was Jepson and Thomas. Jepson was a God-fearing man of unbelievable strength. He had once made a living as a logger and was known to carry twelve-foot cords by himself, one on each shoulder. Once he met Rebecca, he had opened a dairy on the outskirts of town so he could stay closer to home more often. Thomas was Thomas. The Sheriff shook his head to himself as he thought about Thomas. The man was a wild card. He was part everything and yet nothing at the same time. The man could do just about any task you could set him on, but he never hung around long enough to become a tradesman. He was flighty and unpredictable. However, in a fight, he was a pissed off badger. And that suited the sheriff just fine.

The men rode on, kicking up a huge plume of dust, which drifted easterly in the wind. Sheriff Danvers knew their cloud could be seen from a great distance but he hedged his bets on their speed and coverage. He spurred his horse on faster as his mind returned to the fugitive Indian and the justice that must be served.

CHAPTER 23

James had given up trying to figure out where Crouching Bear was hiding. For hours, his mind ached over which direction the man would have gone. Where were there good places to hide? Was it near water for drinking? Would he stay close to game trails in order to eat regularly? Would another town be a good place to hide rather than alone in the wilderness? The questions were perplexing and James had no clear answer to any of them. Instead, he relied on the Indian spirits to guide him to Crouching Bear.

George had tried to override James several times throughout the day. George thought he had the "Injun" figured out. He grew frustrated with James' determination to work through the mystical traditions of the shaman. He implored James to listen to him; first, through ridiculing him for believing in the savage ways; then, by intimidation, using his size and strength as a means to get his way. Finally, he gave in and let James and his horse lead the way.

The two riders crested a hilly expanse and slowed to a stop. They surveyed the plains ahead for anything out of the ordinary. George glanced at James and spat. James ignored George's attention, aware through is peripheral vision that George was looking his way. He was still glad George was accompanying him, but he didn't think he would ever get along with George. And he certainly didn't believe they would ever see eye to eye.

James scouted to the north. His eyes picked up something that he had previously glossed over. About a half mile down the valley, alongside a tributary, it appeared that somebody was standing in plain sight. He squinted to focus in as best he could. It was difficult to discern if it was a man or a lone seedling. His eyes told him it was a seedling. His mind couldn't make heads or tails of it. But his gut told him it was Crouching Bear.

Why would Crouching Bear be caught standing in plain sight? All alone, knowing that lots of folks were hunting him down? If it was him, was he looking for a fight? Would he attack James thinking he had come to avenge the death of Carson's mother? Or would he come quietly, surrendering to James in order to answer for his crime?

George followed James' stare. He sat up higher in the saddle to get a better view. James looked over at George.

"It's him."

"How in hell can you see that far, kid?"

James shrugged. "I can't. I just know."

"Aw, hogwash." George spat a lumpy wad which splashed on the dry soil below. "Ain't no way that Injun juju served him up on a platter for us." His eyebrows came together in exasperation of James' claim.

"It's him, just the same. We'll come in nice and easy. I don't want to scare him into running or doing anything foolish. Just nice and easy."

"And then what? Ya gonna ask him fer a dance? Or pat him on the back fer killing a lady?" George's temper escalated with his tone.

"I'm going to find out what happened and why. Then I'm going to convince him the smart thing to do is to come back to town with us. Otherwise, Sheriff Danvers is going to string him up."

"And what do you think is going to happen to him after you waltz him into town for a trial? Ya really think he won't be swinging then?"

The truth stung James. He hadn't really thought it all the way through. Sheriff Danvers and the posse would certainly hang Crouching Bear out here in the wilderness. It was neat and tidy. No risk of a trial going bad. No spectacle in town of a public trial. No gossip or newspaper press. And, if James did get lucky enough to find the man and convince him to return to town to stand trial, he would certainly be found guilty and sentenced to hang. Somewhere along the way James had believed he would be the hero twice over. Once for capturing Crouching Bear and again for persuading the town to forgive the poor man. He cursed himself for being so childish in his view of the world. Maybe he wasn't ready to be a man after all.

"Doesn't matter what happens later. I want to speak with him and I don't want any trouble until I get the truth."

"Well once you get your truth, I'll be getting my pound of flesh. Eye for an eye." George tilted his brim down.

"You will not touch Crouching Bear at all. This is my call on account it was my idea to come after him. You are supposed to watch over me and nothing else." James surprised himself yet again for standing up to George. He expected George to hand him a beating or, at the very least, a tongue lashing. However, George just fixed his gaze on James. James could feel the heat emanating from the large man. "I appreciate your help but I will not allow anything to get in the way of my mission. Especially, unnecessary violence."

George spat between the horses. "Tell Carson about unnecessary violence when you let him in on yer truth about his momma."

James couldn't argue with George's point. But he still had to find out what happened for his own peace of mind. And he also found he didn't want justice to be handed out by anyone outside the law, which directly contradicted his dreams of adventure and fighting off bad guys. He shook his head again at his naïveté and childish worldview. He realized he had a lot more growing up to do.

"My mission. My call." He confirmed.

George nodded sarcastically. "After you…chief."

James tugged the reins and his horse trotted forward. George's double dig stung him. He was a phony leader of this expedition and he was a tribal leader looking after his braves. It was witty and James recognized it even though it was troublesome. Clearly, George didn't agree with him. He hoped he could figure out how to persuade Crouching Bear to come along peacefully. And how to keep the peace with George.

CHAPTER 24

They saw him. He was sure of it. Crouching Bear felt a sensation in his gut that rolled around, churning. His instincts told him the time had arrived to stand up to the consequences. It happened quicker than he had anticipated. He felt certain he had another day, maybe two, before the face-to-face meeting. Turned out, he completely underestimated James and the power of the vision quest. Of course, he had doubled back toward their direction, so he reminded himself this change in course sped up the process too.

Crouching Bear stood rigid against the breeze and the sun. His long black hair waved behind him. The lines in his face were deep with anxiety. He attempted to defy the spirits by standing firm. It was a somewhat hollow front as he didn't feel completely brave inside. He kept his eyes focused on the horsemen along the ridge line.

The distance between the men was bisected by the kindred connection. Once James' spirit came to him, he felt a deeper pull toward his friend. A link which went beyond their brief friendship. An unseen symbiosis.

The long stare bounded across time and space. He knew he was looking at James. He had no idea who the other man was but he was sure it wouldn't be Carson. He knew James had seen him here too. It was a feeling, a certainty. And he understood the gravity of the situation.

Crouching Bear watched the travelers make their way down the rolling hills. They would be here in less than half an hour. The time to prepare was short. There wasn't much to do but draw from his inner strength to face the men.

Whatever came of this encounter would be written in the heavens by the gods. He knew he was powerless to alter what would come next. But he was relieved to know James would be here soon. As much as he feared the confrontation, he wanted to see his new friend again. The tears welled as he thought once more about how James and Carson took him in and gave him hope for a new beginning.

Crouching Bear bent to the stream's edge to take a sip of water. He saw his reflection in the slow, gurgling currents. It was warped and cloudy, just like his mind felt. The stranger staring back at him reminded him of a time when he ran wild with his brothers. Free to roam across the plains. Hunting for meat and sharing in the kill. Practicing his skills with his hands and his knife. Riding bareback over the hills with the westerly winds against his hair. The fire chats when the elders preached of the spirit world. The stories about the brave ones who came before them. The lessons of honor and loyalty. And, of course, the laughter when the children danced around the flames, tripping over themselves to learn the tribe's way. Those times seemed simpler and freer.

Now he was faced with the prospect of being chained up or dying. The thought of joining the spirits comforted him. Yet he was afraid his warrior soul would be met with disdain, disallowed to fly with the ancients because of his mistakes. His gut told him the answer would come sooner than he cared for.

He scooped a handful of water and slurped it down, the chilly water cooling his body, from his throat down to his belly. He drank several more times before running wet hands through his long, straight hair. The chill seeped through his scalp and cooled him off in the hot sun.

The riders got closer and, with their proximity, the size of their silhouettes grew larger. Crouching Bear couldn't make out the faces yet but the shapes clearly defined the personalities. James bounced high in his saddle, his large ears protruding in the sun; his short, fair hair catching the wind. The second rider was more of a mystery. He could tell the man

CURSE OF THE ANCIENTS

was very large, probably twice the size of James. He wore a cowhide jacket and a large-brimmed dark hat. Crouching Bear ran through the inventory of people he had encountered in the town who would fit the build of the man. The only white man he guessed it could be would be George, the big, nasty man from the saloon. He hoped he was wrong about this guess because, if it was George, Crouching Bear would definitely be in for some trouble. The large man had made it clear during their first encounter he did not like Indians at all, even Indians who had befriended James and Carson.

As he stood up, he unsheathed his knife, feeling the weight of the bone handle in his rough hands. The weight of the knife and the sharpness of the steel comforted him. He couldn't always count on the tribe or his friends, but he could always count on his knife. It would never turn its back on him. Feeling more at ease, he re-sheathed the blade and let his hands fall to his sides. He remained stoic as the pair shortened the distance. The men's faces, coming into view, confirmed it was indeed George and James. Crouching Bear sighed and then stuck his chin higher in the air.

The time of reckoning had arrived. His breath became shallower and stunted in his fear of what might come. He wouldn't let the fear show. He would stand tall and accept the situation for what it was. He made eye contact with George for a long moment, the large man returning a hostile glare. Then he shifted his focus to James. He read confusion in James' light eyes. Crouching Bear wondered what James could possibly be confused about. Wasn't he here to capture Crouching Bear? Or was he here to kill him? He wanted the answer.

CHAPTER 25

The cloud of dust swirled around the horses and took its time dissipating in the warm late afternoon air. The riders remained in their saddles, sitting high above Crouching Bear. The Indian carefully watched the men as if he didn't trust them.

"Crouching Bear." James nodded. He addressed the Indian with a slight croak in his voice, revealing his nervousness. He shifted in the saddle and glanced at George. George sat still until he leaned over and spat a wad of chew at the feet of Crouching Bear.

"Injun." He made no effort to hide his hatred for the man.

Crouching Bear nodded back to James and seemed to ignore George and the tobacco-laden affront.

"What happened back in town?" James paused to swallow. "Did you really do that to Minnie? To Carson's mother?"

Crouching Bear maintained his eye contact with James. "I did."

George slid off his horse and started to approach Crouching Bear. He drew his knife from the sheath on his gun belt. Crouching Bear never flinched.

"Wait." James shouted. "Wait. I told you we needed the truth."

"And you got it, kid. He just said it, with own savage tongue; he killed her. Now he's gotta die."

The sound of a gun hammer cocking echoed behind George. He immediately halted in his tracks, unsure if the boy would use the gun on him.

"I said wait and I ain't gonna say it again." James pointed the pistol at George, who turned to face him. His hand trembled slightly with fear and adrenaline. Everything seemed to be rolling faster than he wanted. His head was dizzy and his stomach butterflies had returned.

"Why, Crouching Bear? Why would you do it?"

"It was not me. But it was me."

George spun toward Crouching Bear. His heavy breathing swelled his chest. He pointed in the Indian's face. "He's telling Injun lies. Lies! He did it. And he has to pay for it."

Crouching Bear shifted his gaze to meet George's. "It was me. But it was neither my hands nor my spirit that killed her."

George smashed Crouching Bear in the nose. The Indian dropped to his knees, blood flowing into his mouth. George managed to control himself a little better after striking the man. He hovered over Crouching Bear but made no other moves to continue hitting him.

Crouching Bear spit blood into the dirt and looked up at George. "The curse was inside me. It came out and made me do it. But I never wanted to hurt that woman."

James lowered the pistol. "The curse? The curse that your tribe gave you? But how?"

The Indian wiped the blood that dripped on his upper lip. "I told you the elders cursed me when they banished me from the tribe. But I didn't yet understand what the curse meant. I knew what it was but not how it would reveal itself."

George kicked Crouching Bear in the stomach and he folded over into the dust. He gasped for air with his knees pulled up to his chest. James jumped down from his horse and ran to George. He grabbed the large man's arm and spun him around.

"What did I tell you? Stay away from him. Now."

George grabbed James by the front of his shirt and tossed him aside. James hit the ground with a thump, exhaling what little air he had in his lungs. Stunned, James lie in the dirt staring up into George's wild, dark eyes. George's teeth were gritted and he was bent forward as he was ready to fight James. James picked himself up and caught his breath for a second before charging George. The surprise of his reaction darted across his mind as he briefly thought how crazy it was he was fighting this huge man who literally scared the crap out of him on a daily basis. The surprise was matched on George's face as he stopped gritting his teeth and his mouth dropped open in awe. James barreled into George's torso as hard as he could. A shock wave ran from his shoulder down to his boots.

George flew backwards into the ground with James on top of him. He quickly punched James in the eye before the boy pulled his pistol from his belt loop. The boy raised the pistol high above his head and slammed the handle down on George's skull. It only took one strike to knock George useless. The large man wasn't unconscious but he was stunned to the point of lying in the dirt and staring up to the skies, eyes searching for purchase. James looked down at his hand and felt like he was unattached from his arm. He grinned as he realized he had used his father's infamous move to subdue someone and the move actually worked. He was proud of himself for a second and then realized George was going to pummel him when he got around to feeling better. James quickly hopped off George and turned to Crouching Bear, who was still on the ground.

"Why? Why would you do that to her? To us?" James realized finally how winded he was and he rested his hands on his knees as he awaited a response.

"It was the anger. If I get angry, the curse turns me into a bear and I attack whoever is before me. I promise you. I would have stopped it if I knew how." Crouching Bear sat up and rubbed his stomach, the blood on his lip drying with dirt sticking to it.

"And what could have made you so angry you would do something to hurt Carson so bad? And me? We were your friends. We brought you to our home even though the whole town wanted you gone."

"I know. I am sorry. I never meant to hurt Carson or you. You are my friends. I didn't want to hurt the woman either. The beast took over. I was not able to stop it."

George was coming around slowly. He sat up but still appeared dazed, his eyes unfocused. Tobacco juice drooled from his lips. He lifted a hand to rub his scalp but missed.

"What am I supposed to do now? The town wants you dead. And we know George wants you dead. Hell, sometimes I think I want you dead."

Crouching Bear was deflated and looked at the earth beneath him. He rested his arms on his knees as he sat.

James huffed and looked around himself. He felt like he was searching for something. For an answer. For a way out of this predicament.

"Maybe we can do something." He scratched his head with the handle of the pistol. He nodded at Crouching Bear. "I might have a plan."

CHAPTER 26

George swallowed some of his tobacco. His face turned a mild shade of green as his stomach fought to right the ship. Then he rolled to his knees, with his arms supporting him. He lifted his head at James then lowered it again with a gasp of air.

James watched George struggle to get up. He started to panic. How was he supposed to handle all this? Things had gone from bad to worse. Moments ago he was chasing down someone he cared for, to bring him to jail for a heinous crime against his best friend's mother. Next thing he knows, he had beaten up a very tough hombre and was fixing to do something even worse by helping his fugitive Indian friend escape. What was he thinking? How could he think of doing something so stupid? Surely, George would whip him and then drag him back to town to publicly shame him. His reputation, the one that didn't really exist, would be tarnished. He'd be thrown in jail or maybe even hung himself. His mother would be thrown out of town, either by the sheriff or by the sheer embarrassment of having birthed such a terrible child. Carson would have to fend for himself. All alone in the world without a mother. Nobody else would care for the boy. They all shunned him and snickered behind his back on account of him being a "retart". They knew he was slow and pretty useless in terms of supporting himself, or his ability to provide anyone else with some type of service. His whole world was upside down and it was going to hell in the high water.

He glanced back at Crouching Bear who had gotten to his feet. The size of his friend had never really occurred to James before. Crouching Bear was not as large as George but he had a formidable stature. Now that he stood face to face with the Indian and came close to wrangling him back to town, James was grateful that George had come along. He knew the prospect of tying the man up and forcing him back to town would no sooner happen than the rapture.

"Uh, we will have to move fast if we are going to make anything work." James turned to George, who was working on stabilizing himself on wobbly legs. "You have to jump on my horse and go back that way." He indicated the route behind him. "You'll find a medicine man in a grove of hackle-berries. He knows about you. And us. You can stay hidden with him until I can get back out there. It might be a few days."

George wobbled over toward James and Crouching Bear. He stammered that he wanted to know what was going on. But then he crumbled back to his knees.

"I cannot run away any longer. I must answer for my actions. The ancients will not accept a coward."

"Forget the dang ancients, will ya? If you wait a few days, I'll bring Carson and the three of us will ride somewhere far away. Someplace where we can start fresh and not have to run or hide."

Crouching Bear crossed his arms in defiance. He stood straight and silent. His gaze never wavered.

"Awww, why does everyone have to be so hard all the time?" James kicked a plume of dust up with his boot. "You aren't giving me much choice here. If you don't get going right now, George is going to whoop us both and then I am going to go to jail and you are going to hang by your neck until you are dead. And Carson will be left to die alone. And my mom will have to whore somewhere else. If she can." James fought the frustration that bubbled up in his gut. He felt the pressure of the seconds ticking away while Crouching Bear remained stubborn. James shifted from foot to foot with impatience and whined liked a little boy. As soon as he whined, he realized he still sounded like a child rather than a grown man out on an adventure. This notion further exasperated him.

George managed to stand up with less difficulty. He leaned to the right and then corrected his posture. His eyes had regained focus and he leered at James.

"You have to go now." James implored Crouching Bear to escape one last time. But Crouching Bear stood still, arms folded. James kicked dirt again and looked at George. George stared him down with disgust.

"Yer one of them, ain't ya?" George took a step closer to the two men. "Yer skin ain't red though. It's yellow." He took another step.

"You better stay right where you are, George. I don't want to hurt you. And I'm sorry I hit you before, but you gotta trust me, okay?"

George looked over at Crouching Bear, who was stiff as a statue. The Indian felt George's eyes upon him and turned to meet his gaze. Both men read each other's intentions. George would not let Crouching Bear escape and he meant to administer his own version of justice on the Indian. Crouching Bear would only go quietly if James led the way. If George laid a hand on him, he would show George what warrior spirit meant. The understanding was apparent between them, yet neither man backed down from the other.

James read the looks between the enemies and knew he had more problems to consider than he had originally anticipated. "Listen to me. Both of you. This is the way it is going to happen. Any other way is the wrong way. Do you understand?" He looked at George who never stopped staring at Crouching Bear. Then he glanced at Crouching Bear who never diverted his eyes from George. "I am warning both of you. I will use this gun if I have to. I don't want to but if you leave me no choice…" The words just hung in the air as he held the pistol in the air.

George charged forward at Crouching Bear. James screamed at him to stop. Crouching Bear kept staring. Not moving. His eyes burning bright red. The air was charged with an energy that caused all three men to take notice. Something was off.

CHAPTER 27

In an instant, Crouching Bear transformed from a man into a bear. James froze in mid-scream. He was stunned that a man could become a beast right before his eyes. It defied everything he knew about the world and he realized seeing was believing. However, it was too late for George. He couldn't stop his momentum as he lunged off the ground at the animal. The horses reared up in fear of the sudden danger.

James was rooted to the ground. He witnessed George crashing head first into the roaring bear. It stood well over seven feet tall, paws outstretched in rage. George bounced off the bear's chest. He hit the earth hard and tried to roll over. But the bear pounced on George's back immediately. It roared and howled as it crushed the man into the dirt. James was awestruck that George looked small compared to Crouching Bear.

He winced as the bear clawed at George's back, tearing through his leather jacket. Stripes of blood formed through the garments. George cried out in anguish as the nails dug through his flesh.

James finally sprang into action. He ran to the fight but he left his gun in his belt loop. He wanted to do his best to stop the battle without having to shoot at Crouching Bear. James hopped on the back of the bear as it tore at George. His hands grasped at tufts of fur, pulling them hard as he struggled to stay on the wild beast's back. Crouching Bear rose and howled at the sky. He jumped off George and thrashed around, attempting to shake James. Two bucks in the air had James flying toward the whinnying horses. He thudded in the dirt and gritted the grains of sand in his teeth. The air completely left his body.

Crouching Bear swung a claw down at James. Even gasping for breath, James managed to roll away from the strike. The claws instead dug earth from the spot where James had lay. Crouching Bear roared at him, spittle flying from the sharp jaws. Suddenly, the bear howled in pain. It stood up and swung its front paws to desperately reach for its back. The massive head turned to find its attacker.

James saw George bent on one knee behind the bear. His left hand was behind his back, trying to hold the wounds. His face was a mask of war. Crouching Bear faced George, and James noticed the large knife lodged in the upper shoulder of the bear. George had stabbed the beast in order to draw it away from James. Unfortunately, George was left without his knife. He pulled his six-shooter from the leather holster at his side. He began to raise the gun at the bear when it sprang on him.

Crouching Bear ripped a hunk of meat out of George's gun hand. George let loose a primal scream and collapsed under the weight of the mighty animal. The pistol dropped to the soil and skittered away as the bear's back paws kicked it. Chewing the bloody forearm meat, Crouching Bear tried to sink his teeth into George's chest. It couldn't make a deadly bite as George wrestled and squirmed to avoid the large teeth.

James ran back to the battle and yanked the knife from Crouching Bear's shoulder. Again, the animal reared in agony as the blade cut deeper on its way out of the furry muscle. James plunged the knife back into the bear. He wanted to stab it low enough to pierce a lung. But the writhing animal moved just enough that James nearly stabbed the same spot on its shoulder. Crouching Bear sounded almost human as he wailed about the new wound. The sound startled James. He gripped the knife tighter and jumped back, slicing more meat as he pulled it out. Crouching Bear swung at James, dragging three claw marks across his neck. The heat burned down the channels of his skin. Blood trickled down his chest. James dropped George's knife and clutched at his neck. He fell to his knees and then collapsed in anguish.

With James out of the fight, Crouching Bear brought his attention back to George. The large man was wheezing. He tried to crawl toward his gun, the front of his shirt, a spreading puddle of crimson. Crouching Bear moved to impede his progress. The bear roared loudly, inches from George's face. The smell of coppery sinew was pervasive. George shielded his face with his mauled arm. The bear stomped on George with all its weight. The force of the animal drove all the air out of George's body. The sound of his ribs crunching made a sickening noise.

James removed his hands from his bloody neck. He peered at the wet stains on his fingers. The wound stung like a hot poker but he realized it was a slight flesh wound. It drew blood but was not enough to kill him. Feeling relieved, James jumped to his feet and ran to the pistol in the dirt. He retrieved it and sprinted to the struggle. He pulled back the hammer on the pistol, emitting a loud metallic click. The sound startled the beast. It swung its body around toward James. His hand shook with fear and exhaustion as the bear came at him. It swung a huge arm, knocking him on the side of his head. His finger squeezed the trigger and a loud crack thundered across the plains. James was unconscious before he hit the ground.

Crouching Bear moaned into his paws. The bullet had shot through his open mouth but exited through the side of his cheek. Blood poured from the gaping hole. The fur on his face was matted down and wet with blood. The great beast writhed in pain. With both men unconscious, the animal took its time tending its wounds. It gathered its strength and loped over to where James lay. His eyes were closed but his gun hand remained up, pointing at the sky as if still aiming the gun. The message had not yet reached the extremities that the lights were out.

Crouching Bear hovered over James' body. He bellowed in anger at the lifeless form. He sniffed the drying scratches upon the boy's neck. Crouching Bear lifted his head to the sun-drenched skies and screamed with victory.

CHAPTER 28

Something had changed. Crouching Bear sensed feelings, for the first time in this form, as an animal. He was suddenly aware of his own thoughts. The thoughts of the man, not the beast. Up until this moment, when he was transformed into the huge bear, everything became instinctual, inhuman. His sense of smell was powerful, able to distinguish food over vast stretches. His hunger was voracious. Never satisfied regardless of how much filled his belly. His mind was mammalian. Only focused on fight or flight. Feeding and hunting. So simple, yet so foreign to the man.

Now that he could think as Crouching Bear, the man, he leaned over James' face. The boy was knocked out and looked so peaceful. Part of him wanted to rip the boy's face off and fill his stomach with protein. The other part of him wept, upset with how he had continued to hurt his dear friend. The balance of human and mammalian brain swung like a pendulum.

Crouching Bear looked down to find he was still the furry animal. His large brown paws and long nails were covered in skin and flesh. He glanced at George. The large man continued to bleed from his chest, the puddle of crimson spreading across his body, the cloud of dust surrounding him slowly settling in the fading sunlight.

He turned back to James. Wrestling with the bear instincts, he took a step back from the boy. His eyes watered over with tears of pity. Crouching Bear thought he had killed the nice boy. James had taken him in, like a family member, when he knew nothing about the man. For all he knew, in the time and place he was raised, all Indians were to be mistrusted and avoided. Still, he welcomed him into the town and then into his family's circle. James had introduced him to his little friend, Carson, and his mother. He withstood ridicule from townsmen and admonishment from George. James had acted as a real friend, never once faltering in the face of adversity. And how did he repay the boy? He killed his friend's mother. He ran off without explanation. He had killed George; although, that was no big loss. And he had probably killed James. He cursed himself silently for the misfortune he had heaped on the only person on the planet that cared for him.

Tears tickled the coarse fur along his snout. He lowered his head in shame. The taste of blood in his mouth disgusted him. He wasn't sure how much of it was his own from the pass-through bullet as opposed to George's flesh. While each being smelled completely different, their blood tasted very much the same.

This curse was far worse than being banished from the tribe. The banishment just meant he was no longer welcome to live amongst his family and friends. But the curse negated any hopes of finding a place to settle. A new beginning. He couldn't have any of it because he would only bring further damnation upon those he encountered. And the shame of his uncontrollable actions, shifting between man and beast, would not allow him the chance to try to start anew.

Crouching Bear began transforming into a man. He felt the burn of his skin as the coarse hairs retracted into his flesh. His jaw snapped inward with a bone-crunching click. The claws drew under his nails, feeding themselves into his bones. The pain was intense. He groaned with each twist and snap. His body becoming more his own again. The mammalian mind receded, bringing more awareness of the horror he had unleashed to the surface.

He was naked. His skin showed splotches of blood stains and filth. Crouching Bear sat up, putting his head in his hands. He cried for Minnie and Carson. He cried for James. He cried for his own miserable existence. He didn't shed a tear for George.

The sun began to move toward the horizon, casting longer shadows upon the destruction. The horses had long since ceased their discomforting whinnying. They grazed on the tall, sunburned grass hundreds of yards from the scene.

Crouching Bear gathered himself. He decided he couldn't stay here. If James and George awoke, they would kill him. His chances of being brought into town for trial had passed with the deadly battle. He stood and stretched his human legs beneath him. His plan for circling back toward his pursuers had not gone as he had anticipated. He knew he had to head in one direction and one direction only. And he couldn't stop. Not until he reached lands where no man lived. That was his only plan now.

He approached George's body. As he looked at the large man, he hoped he had killed him. He hated George as much as George hated him. George never gave him a chance. It would be so easy to finish him in this moment. The man couldn't defend himself so there would be no struggle. But he knew, if he killed George, it would further hurt James. Not because James cared about George. Crouching Bear was pretty sure James liked George about as much as he did. But it would further cement the poor choice James had made in selecting Crouching Bear as his friend. And he knew that guilt would burn inside James forever, which he wasn't willing to risk.

Crouching Bear knelt beside George. He removed George's boots and pants. Tossing the boots aside, Crouching Bear pulled the pants up. He left the gun belt on the ground. He rolled George over and fed his arms through the jacket sleeves. Crouching Bear felt the heavy leather in his hands as he tried it on for size. Like the pants, it was slightly larger than his body but he would make it work. He found his knife near the pile of shredded clothes he used to own. He slid the sheath into the front pocket of the pants. Crouching Bear took one last, long look around at the scene. The two men sprawled in the dirt. The blood spatters staining the weeds and tufts of grass.

He recognized his shame again. Looking down at his bare feet, he knew he must say goodbye to his dear friend James forever. He had hoped they could try to clear the air and he could apologize for his actions. Then he would go peacefully to face his sentence. Instead, he had made everything worse. Crouching Bear walked over to James. He wished he could see his light eyes one more time. But the spirits had decided against it. "I am really sorry, my friend." He choked up a bit.

Crouching Bear leapt over James and ran across the plains toward the setting sun. He hoped his body would keep up until he reached the end of the earth.

CHAPTER 29

The pain seared through James' skull. He heard the blood pounding deep within his ears. The stars above were beginning to shine in the twilight sky. It felt like his eyes were going to pop out of his head and roll down his chest. The pressure was unbearable.

He realized he was lying on the ground and rolled to his side. The shift in equilibrium sparked new bolts of pain in his head. The first thing he saw was the horses. James remembered the horses running off when Crouching Bear attacked. But they must have wandered back afterward. They grazed and snorted in the late afternoon air. George's horse pooped a massive clump as it ate. James closed his eyes at the beginning of a chuckle. He found it humorous that George was like his horse, always spewing something moist and brown upon the earth.

James turned and saw George face-down in the dirt. He scrambled to attend to his companion but slowed immediately as the movement sent shock waves through his brain. The burning on his neck had abated but still stung. He touched the wounds gently with his fingertips, tracing the dried grooves in his skin.

George lie face-down, wearing nothing but his shirt. His hairy ass cheeks mocked the growing shape of the evening's moon. The humor of this situation tickled James again but he squashed his chuckle in fear of sending more bolts across his head. James was afraid to roll George over but he didn't have a choice. As he pulled George's body toward him, he saw the torn flesh peeking through his shirt. He also caught sight of George's shredded forearm as it swung over his rolled body. James was horrified at what he saw. The flesh on George's arm was removed down to the bone. The huge teeth marks ringed the missing flesh. He gently parted the shreds of shirt to check on the chest wound. It wasn't as bad as he would have expected. It appeared to be more of a surface wound as the skin was torn open but the meat was still in place. James felt his companion's neck for a pulse. It was there but it was very faint. George had lost a ton of blood and James needed to get help for him fast.

James grabbed George's gun belt and tied off a tourniquet on his upper arm to stop the bleeding. He ran to his horse to fetch a fresh shirt from his saddle bag. He ran it back over and folded it upon George's chest wound. He used a cord of rope from the bag to tie the shirt tighter to George's chest. It was a struggle to feed the rope under and around the large man's lifeless body but he managed to complete the task. Now he had to figure out how to get George on his horse.

He whistled and both horses trotted over to him. Blowing the air through his lips caused his head to throb harder. How was he going to get this huge guy onto his horse without popping his own head from the strain? James thought fast and sat George up against his body. He tied the long end of the rope which held George's chest bandage in place through the reins of his horse. Then he circled to the opposite side of George's horse. He hopped up over the saddle and pulled the reins to him. The reins came easy at first. Then his arms were met with major resistance as the massive weight of George caught up. He leaned backward, tugging the reins into his chest. George's body lifted a few inches. The veins on James' neck and forearms strained against his skin. The pain in his head was excruciating and it felt like he would black out soon if he didn't get George up. He pulled harder and leaned and George's body came up a little more. James worked himself up to his feet, standing on the far side of the horse's back. The horse grunted and complained. It turned its head toward James in defiance but he struggled on. He leaned further off the side of the horse at an angle that defied gravity, using his own body weight as an anchor, while the ropes pulled over the saddle. George's body came up more, with his lolling head now at saddle height.

James saw nothing but stars. Not the stars that were beginning to reveal themselves in the evening sky. Stars within his eyes from the strain. He puked up a little bile but swallowed it back down. He felt his legs quiver as the blackness closed in around him. He knew he would pass out any second now so he had to go for broke to make this happen. If he couldn't get George over this horse right now, then his friend would certainly die. And he knew he might soon follow as the wildlife would come out at night to feast on his unconscious, defenseless body. James reached down deep in his gut and breathed hard several times. Then he hurled himself off the horse toward the ground with the ropes cutting through his wrists. He hit the ground hard and felt a lightness behind the reins that wasn't there a moment ago. James looked up through starry eyes and saw George three quarters of the way across the saddle. He had done it. James sighed in relief and dropped his head to the ground.

As he caught his breath, James watched the flashes in his eyes drift off. The pounding in his skull lessened but the headache remained. He sat up slowly and rubbed his temples. James pulled himself up and walked over to George's horse. He lifted George's right leg, which dangled from the saddle, and pushed it up higher so his companion was fully stretched over the horse. James tightened the reins and tied the rope to the horn to secure George for the trip ahead.

James collected his pistol from the dirt. He brushed it off and jammed it down his back belt loop. He searched for George's knife and gun. He found the pistol but he couldn't find the knife. James wondered if the knife was still lodged in Crouching Bear. As soon as he had this thought, he realized he had forgotten all about Crouching Bear. The Indian was nowhere to be found and he hadn't even thought about him. He was so worried about helping George and keeping his headache at bay that he totally forgot about his friend.

James fetched George's boots and then searched the horizons for any sign of Crouching Bear, the man or the beast. It was getting darker but there was still enough light in the setting sun that he could see pretty far. The problem was the longer shadows which made discerning distant objects more difficult. He didn't pick up any sign out of the ordinary. James scouted around one more time for George's knife. He found it covered in dirt, sticking out of the soil several yards further away than he had originally searched.

He tucked all the gear into his saddle bag and climbed onto his horse. James spurred the animal and clucked his tongue to signal George's horse to follow along. He knew they had a long trip ahead, through the night. But he had to get George medical attention before it was too late.

CHAPTER 30

Blackness enveloped him. Crouching Bear had to rely on his senses to avoid danger. The plains at night were very dangerous. The wildlife did their best hunting at night. He knew there were coyotes and wolves out here, not to mention the bears. Big bears. Making things even more dangerous was the noise of his movements. He tried to be as stealthy as he could but his exhaustion and injuries made travel difficult. If his tribesmen were nearby, their search would be rewarded with his clumsy running. And who knows how many white men, posse or not, were sleeping on the ground, ready to kill him. He hoped he would find their campfires as a warning sign but he knew dangerous white men, the ones who do evil things, knew better than to burn fires at night.

Crouching Bear's feet were sore from running for so long. He had stepped on many sharp stones and prickly plants he could no longer see in the darkness. Even though his moccasins were made of thin animal skins, they somehow took the edge off the terrain. Those moccasins had exploded off his feet, along with his clothing, when he had transformed into the bear. He felt like a stranger in George's pants and jacket, but at least he would have a little warmth against the chill of the night.

He had to stop to catch his breath. He had been running for several hours now. It would be safer to take a break in the dark than when the sun was up. He dropped to the ground and spread out his limbs beneath the stars.

The moon was half full and left the earth in darkness. Each star shined individually, as if millions of little flames burned in the heavens.

Crouching Bear closed his eyes tight and listened to the night around him. A coyote howled somewhere far behind his head. The breeze dampened the periodic howls every few minutes. He settled into his mind for the first time since he had started fleeing. The vision of James' face was in his eyelids. First James was laughing and telling Crouching Bear about his dreams to travel with Carson and fight bad men. Then James became angry, yelling at Crouching Bear for how he had hurt him and Carson. Crouching Bear winced.

In his heart of hearts, Crouching Bear knew James would keep searching for him. His friend was too strong and too righteous to give up. He would recover from the battle and he would spend the rest of his life hunting down Crouching Bear. The posse would eventually give up when they ached for booze and women. The tribesmen may even give up after some time, focusing instead on staving off settlers and other tribes. They, too, would long for the thighs of their women. But James was different. He would not give up.

Crouching Bear searched his mind for answers. Should he have just killed him? If James were dead, then at least he would be at peace. Of course, the other choice would have been to stay close and await the boy's recovery. Then James could end his miserable life and free him from his curse. He couldn't help but wonder though. Would James pull the trigger? Or would he torture himself more over the choices he would have to make? James would have to kill Crouching Bear, which would take a piece of his innocence away forever. Or he would have to hand Crouching Bear over to the authorities and then watch as the townspeople killed him. The people might or might not resent James for bringing him into the fold to begin with. Or he would have to let Crouching Bear run. Which would further torture his soul for not avenging Minnie's life. And he would be back in the same situation with the townspeople who might or might not resent him forever. James would have to face a very difficult situation regardless of which way it went.

He exhaled deeply into the crisp air. Crouching Bear's sorrow consumed him. He realized he could have saved James all the pain by just waiting for his recovery…and then killing himself in front of James. That way James would not be faced with the decisions of handling the justice or turning him in. And didn't Crouching Bear deserve to wander for eternity without the ancients? Hadn't he deserved his sentence in life or in death? He punched his thigh in frustration.

He sat up and squinted to look around. The night was peaceful so far, but it would not stay that way for long. Crouching Bear knew things would close in around him. He knew James would still come. The spirit connection they now shared told Crouching Bear that James was on his way. He envisioned the boy caring for George. But then he would soon re-dedicate himself to tracking him down. And Crouching Bear knew the next encounter would be the end for one of them. Maybe both of them. He felt it in his marrow. Life would not be fun or easy ever again for him. And now his curse had spread to James. James would be forever tormented by the spirits and their ancient plan as well. The men were tied. Brothers. Forever. In blood.

Crouching Bear jumped to his aching feet. He scanned for danger and then focused his sights westward. He began to run again, having refueled his limbs with rest. His mind continued to berate him for his fall from grace. At least until the endorphins of the run kicked in. Then his mind became one with his body. No more thoughts. All energy directed at balance and stealth and speed. His legs burned but moved across the earth undaunted.

He achieved a rhythmic breathing pattern which increased his capacity to withstand the tired ache of his limbs. The crisp air filled his lungs. A few coyotes barked to the south, signaling either a pack fight or a new meal that would soon be consumed. Crouching Bear closed his eyes and ran on. Allowing the spirits to lead him to where fate would have him. The world quivered at the impending struggle. It trembled beneath his feet. Crouching Bear ignored it and ran.

CHAPTER 31

James couldn't believe how quickly the night had settled in. Back in town, there were a few streetlamps and enough light shining from windows to at least light the way somewhat. Out here, on the plains, it was darker than dark. It was total blackness.

He worried about George. He felt a little different toward the man now that they had fought together. It seemed the battle against Crouching Bear had bonded James to George. After all, as surly as he was, George had saved James from being eaten alive. But even without the battle bond, James couldn't stomach the thought of George getting hurt or dying on his behalf. It was his decision to strike out and search for Crouching Bear. George had only come along because his mother had begged him to watch out for James. And now he was dying because of James.

The horses trotted along in the darkness as best they could. The animals were much more wary of the hidden dangers of night travel than humans. They smelled the snakes and the wolves. They sensed the rough terrain and the shaky footing. So, as fast as James wanted them to go, the horses only went as fast as they were comfortable going.

James had hoped they would run into the posse somewhere along the route. He knew Sheriff Danvers would understand the best way to treat George's injuries. Or maybe one of the other men had training in those skills. He figured they would run into at least some type of camp. People were spread out all over the plains, sure. But he should have seen a fire glowing on the horizon by now. He was beside himself with his poor judgment.

George moaned behind him. James tugged the reins and stopped the horses at once. He slid off his saddle and ran to George. He felt around in the dark for George's neck and found his prickly stubble. His fingers followed the jaw line to his hairy neck and settled upon a throbbing vein. It was still faint, but there.

"George? You there? Say something."

George didn't respond. James leaned closer and felt a slight breath on his cheek.

"Hang in there, George. We're gonna get you fixed up. Hang in there, buddy."

James ran back to his horse with a renewed sense of urgency. He had to find help for George. Yanking harder on the reins, he spurred the horses to a slightly faster pace. George's horse complained as its heavier cargo weighed it down with its uneven load.

Where could we go? James searched his mind for answers. He wished he knew how to handle this situation on his own. It served as another reminder he wasn't as prepared for his adventures as he had thought. He silently yelled at himself for still being a boy, not a man. A real man would have been ready for anything that would have come his way. Food. Shelter. Survival. Anything. But James had run off half-cocked, with some clothes and a knife. He didn't even have a gun until George had given him one. What an idiot he had been.

He spurred the horses into a bit more of a gallop. George's horse complained more forcefully this time. The horses had eaten well and drank from the tributary after the men fought. But they didn't rest very long considering how many miles they had logged today. James now began to worry if the dang horses would survive his stupidity too.

It hit him like a lightning bolt. The medicine man. That's where James could go. If he didn't find any camps soon, he could head back to the medicine man's place. Surely, he was versed in the healing of a man.

If he could fly James to Crouching Bear through his mind, then patching up some wounds shouldn't be too hard. Although, George's wounds were pretty severe, he reminded himself. It's not like George had a twisted ankle or a broken finger or even the squirts. George was missing most of his right arm. And his chest looked like a bloody bowl of stew. Not to mention all the blood that he had lost.

James strained to follow the right direction. It was tricky in the absolute darkness. But he followed the stars the way they had taught him in the schoolhouse when he was a little fella. He just had to locate the North Star and then he could figure out all the cardinal directions from there. So he did the best he could as he bounced up and down in the saddle.

His mind began to shift further into the future. What would happen once he got George to Soaring Eagle? Would the Indian help them? He wondered if his assumption was too optimistic. And, if Soaring Eagle helped them, then what would they do? Could George even survive his wounds? And if he did, how long would it take George to recover? Then where would they go? Would they continue on, searching for Crouching Bear? Or would it be wiser to head back to town, alive but unsuccessful? And when they got back to town, what would happen? Would they lock George and him up for going out on their own against the sheriff's orders? Would Filler take George back as a bouncer in the saloon after he walked out on him without notice? Could James and his mother remain in town or would they be cast out for bringing Crouching Bear into their home? And what about poor Carson? His little buddy. Would Carson know by now the truth behind his mother's absence? Would the town hold true to their word about hiding her death from the little boy? How would he ever face Carson for lying to him? For withholding the truth? He felt ashamed for being such a terrible friend.

James realized he was crying. His heart ached with how badly he had betrayed everyone he cared about. It was all his fault and the harm was spreading around. Minnie. Carson. Crouching Bear. His mother. Now George. He wondered when it would end. It could only end with him finding Crouching Bear.

James squeezed his eyes against the breeze and leaned forward in the saddle. He had to get George to Soaring Eagle. Time was running short.

CHAPTER 32

Murphy threw another log on the fire. Sparks of ashes splashed the night air, fizzling in the breeze. Sheriff Danvers removed his hat and ran a hand through his curly hair. His back ached something fierce from the long ride. Years of riding and fighting were taking their toll on his body. At thirty-five, he was still fairly young but the miles on his frame told a different story.

The men had decided to settle in for the night. They were all tired and cranky. The horses had become more ornery too. Sheer darkness closed in around the small team huddled near the fire.

Jepson read his bible aloud. He offered to fill the silence as the men choked down dried meats and celery. Nobody had minded. The men were too tired to even respond. As Jepson read from the Old Testament, Thomas snored gently under the brim of his hat. His feet rested on some piled wood. Hannigan was picking his nose and raised one leg to pass wind. Jepson paused in his reading, shooting Hannigan a harsh look for showing disrespect for the Lord's words. Murphy chuckled while he warmed his hands over the flames.

Sheriff Danvers leaned back against his saddle bag. He gazed upon the starry sky, wondering what life would be like if he could reach the heavens. He thought to himself that it must be so beautiful up there. Peaceful. And no need to chase down fugitives. His career was long enough to span dozens of manhunts. Most of them were led by him, and he had ridden along on a few more with other sheriffs. All manhunts were the same. One man would run as far as he could until the posse caught up with him. It was inevitable. The fugitive would run out of water or food and have to make a last stand. They either died in their boots or were captured and brought to justice. Danvers had never lost a fugitive, nor had he personally known of one who got away. Of course, there were the legends of famous outlaws who escaped the clutches of the law. He knew there were exceptions to the rule. But they were few and far in between. Part of Danvers feared this particular manhunt.

This chase was different. An Indian was a savage animal. Accustomed to living in the wild, able to withstand the elements. A white man was anchored by his habits. Once a man knew the comforts of a bed and food and the warmth of a woman's body, the desire to stay the course easily wavered. It was only a matter of time until the man's psyche caved. The walls of one's own mind pressing in were far more valuable to the chase than the most skilled posse. All the posse had to do was stay on the trail and stay close. The fugitives did all the work themselves, through human weakness.

Danvers rolled a cigarette. He liked to puff away a bit before closing his eyes. The tobacco soothed his mind, which in turn gave his body permission to shut down. Being a sheriff, a man had little time to relax. Something was always amiss or there was need for representation; a presence at a meeting here, a bunch of handshakes at a gathering there. His job was round the clock and he preferred that. His soul was restless and being so active kept him rooted. Otherwise, he would have jumped on his horse and ridden around the world one hundred times by now.

As he blew a cloud of smoke into the sky, Sheriff Danvers thought about the Indian. Several things worked against the Indian's chances. First off, he was on foot which would make it quicker to catch up to him. Second, he had nowhere to run to. His tribe had booted him out and he couldn't go back to town. So he would have to run and keep on running. Of course, these factors just might work in the Indian's favor too. Being on foot, it would be harder to track his movements. Horses always left tracks. There was no avoiding it. But a man on foot could conceal his trail better. And with nowhere to run to, the possibilities for his whereabouts were limitless. As long as his legs carried him, the Indian could head in any direction and travel to the ends of the earth.

His gut warned him he was dealing with something far more dangerous than he was accustomed to. He couldn't reconcile the cannibalism. Sure, he had heard tales of Indians eating white men or crazy mountain men who were forced to eat human flesh to survive. But this was too close to home. That Indian had not only killed that poor working girl, he had eaten her. Only bones and some meat were left behind. That made this fugitive that much more dangerous. He ate someone when he wasn't even starving or trying to survive. A chill slithered down his pant leg as he tossed the remnants of his cigarette into the fire.

Jepson closed his bible and said goodnight. Nobody responded. He rolled over and pulled a blanket over himself. Hannigan snored louder than Thomas. Murphy watched the sky with his arms folded behind his head. Sheriff Danvers laid back and propped his hat over his face. The smell of the tobacco on his beard filled the small opening around his nose. He heard a prolonged fart from one of the men. Then silence.

Danvers closed his eyes and pictured sitting on his porch with his dog, Shooter, at his feet. He smelled Laurie's apple pie wafting from the window. He was looking forward to a relaxed retirement life to wait out his days. He would enjoy his cigars and reading those Shakespeare histories he had enjoyed as a schoolboy. His hopes and dreams were disturbed by visions of violence and bloodshed. The apprehension of an indefinable evil clouded his pleasant repose. A sense of foreboding filled him as he tried to block out the scenes from his mind. He couldn't help but feel that he might not make it home from this manhunt, let alone live long enough to enjoy the retirement of his dreams. He rolled to his side and knew he wouldn't be sleeping tonight. He cussed into his hat. "Aw, shit."

The words fell on deaf ears as all the men slept. Except for the sheriff. Instead, he used his time to plot through the next day's moves. He had to catch that Indian bastard. He had to catch him very soon.

CHAPTER 33

Crouching Bear squeezed between a few hackle-berries. It was dark and he thought this grove would provide some cover for him to rest for a few hours. He would only allow himself to take a short breather before putting more miles behind him, under cover of night.

The hairs on the back of his neck pricked up. He suddenly felt a presence. He squatted down and sniffed the air. His senses picked up a fragrant brew that his people would use as a sleep aid. It was a unique blend of herbs and cinnamon. The smell was faint but undeniable.

A soft clicking sound on his right caught his attention. It reminded him of an old Indian game that parents played with their children. The parents would hide and the children had to search for them. When the kids got close, the parents would make a clicking noise to let them know they were nearing their location. It doubled as a safety mechanism, signaling 'friend' as opposed to 'foe'. A foe would remain silent to spring upon the child and harm him.

Crouching Bear quietly crawled toward the spot the clicking came from. As he felt his way through a thicker patch of undergrowth, he heard a voice speak in his tribal dialect. It was almost a whisper but loud enough for Crouching Bear to identify. His heart stopped. Only an Indian would know how to speak the language. Could this person be one of the warriors searching for him? Had he been so careless as to wander right into his own death trap?

Crouching Bear took a chance, figuring he would be dead either way. Inside this thick grove in the pitch black night, his chances of outrunning the warriors were not good. So he returned the clicking noise.

A flame of fire flashed a few feet in front of him. The light was so bright that Crouching Bear could do nothing but squint against it. Another Indian sat across from him, holding a lit match used by the white man.

Soaring Eagle had welcomed him into the circle. The dense foliage provided a backdrop to hide the bright flames from distant eyes. A small opening in the hackle-berries above allowed the smoke to drift up into the starry sky.

Crouching Bear sat by the fire and chewed a dirty root that the elder had offered him. Its taste was bitter but it gave him sustenance. He studied the old man's wrinkled face as he toiled with wrapping some tea leaves. Crouching Bear chose not to reveal why he was traveling alone at night. He also avoided the old man's inquiries about tribal affiliation by complaining of his aches and pains. The old man shifted from his questions to preparing a brew.

"You are running from something."

Crouching Bear stopped chewing and swallowed the mouthful of root. The old man spoke as he worked the tea leaves, never glancing up.

"I see this in your eyes. And your wounds."

Crouching Bear raised his hand to the wound on his cheek. He glanced down at the blood stains on his chest and stomach. The bleeding from his shoulder had stopped but the stains remained. As he looked down at the splotches, he also realized he was wearing George's clothing. Another dead giveaway that he was involved in something beyond normal business. Crouching Bear sighed to himself for being so careless.

"It is okay. You are safe here. For now. I have no disagreement with you." Finally, the old man raised his eyes to Crouching Bear. "I have seen these garments before."

Crouching Bear's heart seized in his chest. If he had seen George's clothes, this must be the shaman who had helped James go on his vision quest. It had to be him. Who else in this vast wilderness was there that had the skills and knowledge to help James? This old man was helpful and nothing like the other tribesmen that lived in the region.

"Angry white man wore clothes just like that very recently. Maybe he is no longer amongst the living?"

Crouching Bear shrugged. "I do not know. The white man wanted to take me to his village and I had to do what was necessary to survive."

"So you are the one they were searching for. You are Crouching Bear."

He was stunned when the old man used his name. Things had taken a surreal twist yet again. Crouching Bear was amazed with the ancients' ability to force a man to remember his place in the universe. He nodded in acknowledgment.

"The boy is your spirit bond. You will not outrun him." Crouching Bear looked down. "There is a way to release you from the curse of your elders."

He sat up and waited impatiently for the old man to finish pouring the brew into an earthen cup. He accepted the cup and felt the heat on his hands.

"A battle must be fought. A battle where one man will die." Soaring Eagle sipped from his cup. "You must kill the one with the spirit bond."

Crouching Bear's excitement deflated. Fighting James was the last thing he wanted to do. Now the old man told him he must kill James to remove the curse. Again, he was plagued with the decisions he must make. He really wanted to release the curse. But he had no stomach for doing more damage to his friend.

"Why? Why must I kill James? He has done nothing but show kindness to me. I have hurt him and those he loves. Why would I choose to do more harm?"

Soaring Eagle rested his cup on a flat stone. He rubbed his calloused hands together with a scratching sound. "The boy has committed to protecting you. He drank from the oils to find you, knowing he would forever be bound to you. The only way to remove the bond, brought about by the curse, is to kill him. With one act, the bond and the curse will be broken."

"I cannot do it."

"He is a white man. The spirits do not care about the white man. The spirits worry about your soul. The only way to join the spirits now is to break that bond."

Crouching Bear nodded, not in agreement but acceptance. The old man was wise and well versed in the ancient traditions. He spoke truth. But Crouching Bear was no fool. He knew, even if he defeated James, he would still be an outcast. A man with no tribe. A man with no village. A man with no friends, and on the run forever. The curse of the bear would be gone, but the curse of not belonging could never be lifted.

He made up his mind. Nothing would deter Crouching Bear from doing what he had to do.

CHAPTER 34

James was close. He knew they would soon reach the shaman's grove. They had traveled for several hours. Slowly, as far as he was concerned. But he could only go so fast with George's injuries and two tired horses. James yawned as the exhaustion tried to overtake him.

He had to stop several times to check on George. The man still had a faint pulse. His bleeding had stopped thanks to the tourniquet and the shirt-bandage. But James kept wondering how long his friend could fight off the hands of death. He chuckled to himself at the thought of considering George a friend. After George saved his life, James had only thought about the positive aspects of the big guy, his fighting skills and loyalty. Well, at least to James' mother. He even found some of his quirks sort of funny now when he used to hate them. Things like always spitting and missing the spittoon. Or his colorful language. Or his overall hardness. In a way, it could be charming and folksy. Maybe not.

James heard his stomach gurgle. The men hadn't eaten since earlier in the day. Much earlier. He wasn't used to going so long in between meals. The one benefit of working in the saloon was he got three squares a day. The meals weren't always tasty, and with the exception of breakfast, he had to eat out on the porch like a dog. But there were three meals nonetheless. And he always got to eat with his pal, Carson. The thought of Carson made James really homesick. He missed his mother but Carson was like his shadow. Always there. Bumping into him. Hanging onto his shirttail. Dogs weren't man's best friend. Carson was.

He wondered what Carson was doing at this hour. The ladies would be working so who was watching Carson? Was he eating on the back porch all by himself? Was he tucked into the hiding spot, alone in the dark? James hated himself for leaving the boy behind. It was for Carson's own protection but so much about this adventure left James guessing about why he had made such a bad choice.

As they crested the rise, James could make out the hackle-berry grove jutting into the flatlands. It was a good distance ahead and hardly perceptible to the naked eye. The only reason he could barely see the grove was because he knew it existed. If a stranger happened by, they would never know the stand of trees was there. They were invisible, yet visible.

James felt a renewed energy burst forth as he knew the end was near. He clucked and spurred the horses on. They complained but picked up the pace slightly. The horses were out of gas as much as the men were. George moaned as his body bounced harder due to the quickened pace.

He was afraid of startling Soaring Eagle. He knew the Indian lived there because it was remote and hidden, and afforded him plenty of protection against critters and white men. James whistled loudly as they galloped close so Soaring Eagle would know to expect visitors without having to unsheathe his knife.

James could smell the fire burning but there wasn't a stitch of light shining in or around the grove. It was an amazing hiding spot and James thought about using similar aspects of this grove for the spot he and Carson shared. It would be a fun project for them to work on and it would further solidify their hideaway.

As they reached the stand of trees, James whistled again. He spoke loud enough for Soaring Eagle to hear him without his voice carrying too far on the wind.

"Soaring Eagle, it's James. I need your help."

Soaring Eagle held up a hand and stopped speaking. His eyes narrowed as he listened carefully. He had heard a whistle while he was speaking to Crouching Bear, but he couldn't be sure if it was human or a bird. It was unlikely for a bird to be whistling at this hour, as most of the winged creatures would have already gone to sleep for the night. Only the hunting birds would be awake at this hour and those birds didn't whistle.

He heard it again. It had a sing-songy cadence to it and definitely came from human lips. Before he could stamp out the fire, Soaring Eagle heard a voice. It called out to him. It was James asking for help. He glanced over the flames at Crouching Bear, who had recognized the boy's voice. Crouching Bear jumped to his feet, grabbing his knife. Soaring Eagle waved him off.

"You must face the boy but this isn't the right place. You must travel toward the setting sun. You will find a grove of weeping willows. There you will prepare for your battle."

Crouching Bear looked down at his knife. He re-sheathed it and thanked Soaring Eagle for his hospitality and wisdom. As Crouching Bear made his way through the dense foliage at the rear of the grove, Soaring Eagle took a deep breath. He thought about the ancients and their master plan. They had cast him right in the middle of this battle. A day ago he was living peacefully, alone in his little paradise. And now he was both the adviser and the instigator to a pair of men. He refused to rebel against the wishes of the spirits. He had learned long ago that the spirits would get their way regardless of what man did to alter the course.

He closed his eyes and breathed deeply. The scent of blood was thick in the air. He knew from Crouching Bear's dress that the cranky white man would be in need of attention. James had brought the man to Soaring Eagle to save his life. The cranky white man could not be in very good shape. He arranged some medicinal herbs and large leaves for poultices. Then he rose to meet James beyond the walls of the hackleberries. The cranky white man was very large and James would need all the help he could get to bring the injured man into the circle.

147

CHAPTER 35

James sat down like a leaden weight. His body hit the ground with a thud and he tilted back. Thankfully, getting George off the horse was much easier than hoisting him onto it. Soaring Eagle had met James outside the grove. He had helped James carry George into the grove. It was slow and difficult but they had managed to get the large man inside.

Soaring Eagle got to work immediately on some medicinal poultices which he applied to George's wounds. The chest wounds were messy but shallow. The old man stitched some aloe fibers through the skin to draw the flaps together. He also wrapped a goat-hide tightly around George's torso to support his fractured ribs. Soaring Eagle had counted five broken ribs, tracing his fingers along George's sides. And those were just the ones he could feel. He told James there might be several more with tiny fractures or cracks. George's forearm was a disaster. A huge chunk of flesh was missing and part of the bone was exposed. Soaring Eagle found a tooth mark scratched into the forearm bone, signaling just how deep Crouching Bear had bitten him.

James rubbed his temples. His head still ached from the blow he took. His massive headache had never gone away; it had only ebbed between painful and extremely painful. Soaring Eagle was brewing a tea which was supposed to get rid of his headache. While the tea was on the fire, Soaring Eagle continued to work on George's arm. The old man had a protein paste he used to fill in the missing flesh. Every few seconds he would pat the mixture heavily to pack it into the gaping hole. He told James it was a mixture of smoked pig meat and some sort of plant that he couldn't remember the name of. It was supposed to aid in the healing of severe burns and provide a protective skin when it dried. Even though George wasn't burned, Soaring Eagle hoped the salve would work just the same for this type of injury.

James closed his eyes and fell instantly asleep. The exhaustion carried him beneath the plane of the waking world.

James opened his eyes. He shot up instantly when he saw Soaring Eagle sitting next to the fire. The events of the day flooded his mind and he panicked that he had not taken care of George.

"Relax. Everything is under control."

James exhaled. He saw George bundled up under animal furs and close to the warmth of the fire. His skin was ashen. His cheeks looked sunken. "Is he going to be okay?"

"It is too soon to tell. He has a chance. If you hadn't gotten him to me by the time you had, he would have had no chance at all."

James rubbed his forehead. He still had a bad headache but he felt a little better after sleeping. "How long was I out?" It felt like hours since he had walked into the circle.

Soaring Eagle finally looked at James. "Only a few minutes."

James shook his head in disbelief. He felt like he had slept for a long time. Soaring Eagle laughed at James' reaction. He stretched an arm over the flames to hand James the cup of tea. "Drink."

James took the hot cup and blew on the tea. He sipped slowly and grimaced at the harsh flavor. "Ugh, this tastes like a ten-day old cow patty in a swamp." The odd phrase got Soaring Eagle laughing again. James smiled and then sipped again. This time more quickly and without breathing through his nose to avoid the horrible taste.

"How did your search go?" Soaring Eagle's tone suggested sarcasm as he nodded toward George.

"Not good. We found Crouching Bear. He and George fought. It was the scariest time of my life." James placed the empty cup at his feet. He stared at the flames. "I almost died but George saved me."

The old man tossed a few sticks into the fire. Wisps of hot ashes popped and fizzed into the air. "The curse is very powerful. It does not care who is hurt by it."

James reflected on the last two days and how much had changed. Everything had been set in motion by Crouching Bear's curse. As much as he had always dreamed of his fantasy adventures, he suddenly wished this one had not come true. He handed the cup back to Soaring Eagle. "I don't know what to do."

The old man busied himself with cleaning the cups and arranging the next batch of poultices. James watched him work. The old man's hands were so sure, almost graceful in their movements.

"You must face Crouching Bear and end the curse." He glanced at James. "He will be expecting you."

"How do you know that? Did you drink some of that magical potion and fly to him too?"

Soaring Eagle stopped working. He sighed slowly and then leaned toward James. "He was here. We spoke."

"What? Crouching Bear knows you? But how? When did you see him?"

Soaring Eagle's eyes narrowed, the lines of age drew wider. "Moments ago. He wanted help. Like you. I help everyone in need."

James was dumbfounded. He had chased Crouching Bear all across the plains and he had just missed him. And, right here, of all places. James slapped his knee in frustration. "Well why didn't you tell me when I got here? I coulda grabbed him and ended this whole thing."

"You would not have been ready." Soaring Eagle crawled over to George and began replacing poultices. He worked while he spoke, with his rear facing James. "You needed to concentrate on helping George. And you needed to get your energy back." He silently worked for a few minutes while James stewed. "You would have died."

"Nobody is going to die. I am going to grab him and bring him home so he can answer for his crimes. He is my friend but he has to pay for what he did." James emphasized his points with anger.

The old man turned and dropped his rear to the dirt. "One of you must die in order to release the curse."

The words hit James like an iron shovel. He began to protest the old man's theory but stopped before uttering a word. His stomach sank. In his gut, he knew what Soaring Eagle told him was true. James pondered the potential outcomes and grimaced at each conclusion. He stood up and dusted off his pants.

"I must be on my way. But what should I do with George?"

"He will stay here. I will see to his care. You must go and follow the trail that fate has laid before you."

James nodded. He looked at Soaring Eagle and then at George. He had to end this curse before more people got hurt. Even if one more had to die.

CHAPTER 36

Sheriff Danvers watched from the hill crest. Down below, beyond the yellowed grass, an Indian gutted a fish. Every few seconds the Indian would stop working to check the landscape for followers. Danvers thanked the dear Lord for this stroke of luck. The fugitive must have been so hungry he had stopped to have a meal. The sheriff felt a little disappointed that the Indian was just as weak as a white man. Somewhere in his mind, he had hoped for a little challenge, a new twist on the game of manhunt.

The sheriff was low to the ground. He had removed his hat and crawled to the top of the hill before letting the posse cross over. He was grateful now that he had. He watched Crouching Bear from between tall blades of dried out grass plants. Without taking his eyes off his quarry, Sheriff Danvers whispered to the men behind him.

"Hannigan. You and Thomas head northwest. Follow the ridge line about two hundred yards and then cut down on my signal."

"With pleasure, boss man." Both men jogged behind the slope.

"Jepson, Murphy. Take the southwest side and stay low. The banks of that stream won't hide you for long. So be careful. When I signal, you come at him."

Jepson replied with a "Yessir," while Murphy snickered. They scrambled across the slope.

Danvers watched the fugitive eat. In between bites, the Indian scoured the horizon for movement. His nerves had finally kicked in, making him a little jittery. The situation was going to require some finesse. Even though they had the high ground, the Indian had the advantage of wide sight lines. His position, while exposed, gave him ample time to flee in whichever direction suited his escape. He worried about his choices of men now. He had chosen the posse based on needs for tracking and brute strength. Toughness, too. But what his men possessed in these abilities, they lacked in stealth. The Irish boys were as clunky as a pissed off mule. They could take a beating as much as they could dish one out. But they were noisy sons of bitches. Jepson was big and lanky, not easily hidden in this environment. Thomas might be his ace in the hole.

He quickly glanced right to follow the progress of Hannigan and Thomas. The men had reached the mark and were poised for his signal. The Indian seemed to have slowed down now that he had a full belly. He sucked the bones for scraps of meat. Danvers checked the left flank as Jepson and Murphy got close to their mark.

Now he had to choose the right moment for the maneuver. Depending on what the Indian was doing when he gave the signal, Danvers would send one team in. The Indian would more than likely balk in the opposite direction, at which time Danvers would signal in the other team. The four men would cordon off most of the escape routes. The Indian would then fall right into his trap by coming his way. Or he would have to fight through the enclosing net. The savage may be strong enough to take on two men, but four would be a huge feat. And, if he got his own hands dirty, well then, Danvers liked his chances even better. He quietly thanked the Lord again for this chance to end the hunt smoothly. If he could just keep his men from getting too busted up, he would be happy.

The Sheriff's eyes grew wide when he watched the Indian move. Could this really be happening? Of all the possibilities he had imagined when planning this hunt, he never would have guessed he would be seeing what he was this very second. The red man was taking off his clothes. He stripped down to his raw nature and began wading in the stream. Danvers wanted to laugh out loud at his good fortune but contained himself. Just barely. This would be the break they needed. With the Indian as naked as a jaybird, no weapons within reach, he was a dead goner. There would be no way for him to react upon seeing the men charge him. By the time he could get up the bank and gather his belongings or reach for a knife or something, he would be surrounded by men. This could not have gone any better. Danvers praised God above.

The Indian dunked himself under the icy waters of the stream. The sheriff waved his hat to his left, sending in Jepson and Murphy first. He had anticipated sending the other two first but the Indian had his back to the men downstream so they would be able to move within range much quicker before detection. This improved their chances. Jepson caught the signal and tapped Murphy on the shoulder. The two men drew their pistols and ran toward the Indian's location, keeping low as they went.

Sheriff Danvers scratched his dark curly hair and smiled at this unexpected fortune. He watched as his men got within fifty yards or so and then he waved his hat at Hannigan and Thomas. Both men moved quickly down the hill, Hannigan with his lever-action rifle and Thomas with a pistol in hand. The sheriff placed his hat on his head and began his own trek, down the hill, toward the stream. He bent forward to stay out of sight as long as he could. They had the savage surrounded and it would all work out, just like it was supposed to. Sheriff Danvers had made a reputation for bringing justice down on those who failed to abide by the laws. His perfect record on posses would remain intact, further cementing the legend of his authority.

As he ran down the slope, Sheriff Danvers pictured returning home to his wife, Laurie, and his dog, Shooter. He saw the streets lined with cheering townsfolk as he marched to the jail with his prisoner in shackles. There would be clapping and rounds of drinks at the saloon, none of which he would enjoy. But his men would soak in the glory of a successful bounty. The Mayor would issue a proclamation with his annoying, bushy white mustache dancing over his chubby lips. It would be well deserved for a job well done.

He fixed his eyes on the Indian as he dunked himself under the water again. His legs moved faster while he was free to stand taller in his gait. Danvers pulled his six-shooter from its holster. The Indian broke the surface of the water, looking right at him as he came down the hill. The look on his face told Danvers that the surprise attack had worked.

CHAPTER 37

Crouching Bear felt full. The fish he had caught wasn't large, but, after eating next to nothing over the last day or two, it seemed like a big meal. He was more satisfied and his nervousness had faded. As he cupped some water to his lips to wash down the food, the cool silkiness of the water dripped through his fingers. He wished he could swim in the crisp waters and further soothe his restless soul. The fields were empty so he jumped at the chance to enjoy himself for a moment.

He removed the leather jacket and then slid the dungarees down around his ankles. Crouching Bear lifted each foot separately to shake off the pants. He walked right into the stream without regard for the drastic temperature change. It felt so refreshing. For the first time in as long as he could remember, he felt free. What was it about floating in water that made a man lose himself? Lying back, he kicked his feet gently as the icy water ran between his toes. The feeling of cleanliness was a luxury men on the plains did not enjoy often. Being landlocked for the most part, the lands were unforgiving. Dry and hot. But this was like walking in the clouds.

Crouching Bear sunk under the current; the water was flowing gently at his chest and moving his manhood freely between his legs. He stretched his arms out to the side to catch the push of the current heading downstream. It reminded him of his childhood when the boys would roughhouse in the waters on hunting trips. The men would let the boys play in the streams to forget the failed hunts. If they couldn't bring meats and furs back to the village, they would have play time. With animal meat, there would be no time for delay. The party would have to get the meat cleaned and back to the village for curing.

As he came up, the sun warmed his face. Rivulets of water poured down his cheeks. He gulped some water and spit it out in a flume like he had done as a boy. The water also shot out the side of his mouth, through the bullet wound. He didn't care. A smile spread across his face. His curse was almost forgotten. For the moment, Crouching Bear was happy. He sunk under the water again.

When he rose from under water, Crouching Bear saw a man running down the hill, toward the stream. The man had a black hat with long curly hair, and a gun in his hand. Crouching Bear knew he was with the posse from town. He turned to head to the shore. As he spun, he saw two more men headed down stream, coming his way. All three men were within shooting distance. He swam as fast as he could to the bank of the stream. He reached the shore and clawed his way up the bank, turning the dirt to mud. Out of his peripheral vision, Crouching Bear noticed two more men coming up stream. He was surrounded. There would be no way out of this mess, unless he fought his way out. His anger at being caught off guard spiraled up his spine.

The men shouted for him to surrender. But his rage flared deep within his belly. The sounds of his bones stretching, cracking with transformation, startled the approaching posse. He felt millions of hairs sprouting through his pores. Claws extended from the pads on his paws. Crouching Bear became the beast once again. He stood on his hind legs and roared at the two men coming down stream. The man with the pistol filled his britches; the bear picked up the overwhelming odor. The one with the rifle stopped and took aim. Crouching Bear approached the shooter as he cocked the lever. The man fired a shot which just grazed the chest hairs under his heart. Crouching Bear swung an enormous paw and lopped the head clean off the shoulders. The headless body still clutched the rifle as it tipped over.

A bullet struck Crouching Bear in the back, spraying blood. He lunged forward, landing on the man with all the droppings in his pants. Crouching Bear clamped down on his face and tore the skin straight up. The man howled in anguish as he grasped at what used to be on the front of his head. The terrifying shrieks scorched Crouching Bear's ears. He bit down on the man's throat, flooding his maw with gushing blood. The man died instantly.

Another shot missed him and he turned on all fours. The two men heading up stream were firing bullets from their pistols. The man with the red hair knelt on one knee. The taller of the two stood and fired. Crouching Bear charged the men as bullets continued to rip through the air on either side of him. The tall man kept pulling his trigger but no more bullets came. He had fired all his rounds and did not stick around to reload. He threw the handgun at the bear and ran for his life, screaming at the top of his lungs. Crouching Bear kept charging the kneeling man. As he got closer, he noticed how ruby red the man's hair was. His eyes were cold. He laughed as he kept firing, holding his ground. Crouching Bear landed on top of the red-haired one. Thrashing and scratching, the bear dug deep grooves into the man's chest and stomach. He pulled intestines out with his powerful jaws, filling his mouth with many tasty fluids.

The bear looked left, up the rise, and watched the black hat man stare in horror. His pistol remained at his side as he watched his friend get eaten alive. The blood-soaked shrieks gurgled as the man drowned in his own liquids. Crouching Bear taunted the black hat man, howling in his direction, chunks of skin flying from his open mouth. The black hat man was visibly shaken. His lips quivered through his thick beard. Another roar sent the black hat man scrambling back up the hill. Without a sound, the man ran and leapt his way to the crest.

Crouching Bear let loose a victorious scream which thundered through the valley. The echo sounded louder when it traveled back to his ears. He ate heartily, filling his belly with more meat than he needed. He was insatiable, not letting anything go to waste.

Crouching Bear thought to himself as he chewed his food. He was completely himself now in the bear's body. It was he who invoked the anger. It was he who killed the men. It was he who ate the flesh of a fellow human being. The bear no longer controlled him. He was in control of the beast. As one body. One spirit. One monster.

CHAPTER 38

Dust blew into his mouth, along with a winged insect. James gagged and spit the bug out. He retrieved his canteen and swished water to clean his mouth. As he put the canteen back in his bag, he noticed two riders coming his way from the west. James could see that they were coming fast and he wondered if he should take cover or wait to question them about signs of Crouching Bear.

The riders got closer and James saw that it was Sheriff Danvers and Mr. Jepson. He figured they were on posse but he was confused why it was just the two of them. Why were they headed back toward town? Why were they riding so fast? A posse searching for a man would surely ride a little slower to look for signs. James sat back in his saddle and awaited the men as they came up to him.

"Ho." Sheriff Danvers reined in his horse and pulled alongside James. Mr. Jepson took longer to slow his horse down. James got the feeling that Jepson didn't intend to stop at all but then thought better of it.

"What are you doing here, James?" The sheriff looked like a man in panic. Something about his face appeared aged or worried. James couldn't figure it out but he sensed something was wrong.

"Uh, well, I want to find Crouching Bear. Before he hurts more people."

Jepson screamed a string of obscenities and almost indiscernible babble. James tried to follow along but it only added to his confusion.

"Shut yer damn mouth." Sheriff Danvers showed frustration with Jepson. "Son, ain't no way you are going to stop that Indian. You'll be killed. He just slaughtered my men a few miles back." The sheriff caught himself from choking up, his eyes reddened and watered. "That Indian became a bear. Right before our very eyes." He rubbed his beard. "I can't even explain what it was." He was clearly shaken.

James felt sorry that he knew more about the curse than the folks from town. He was afraid of the sheriff's reaction but he owed the man an explanation.

"Crouching Bear was cursed by his tribe elders, sir. He came to our town to escape his tribe. He can't control it. It is more than anyone can understand, including Crouching Bear."

Danvers blinked rapidly. "Nobody knew that. We should have known that." James looked down with shame as the sheriff yelled at him. "Ain't no amount of men to take that Indian down. He's too much for us. We're heading home and we ain't coming back. That Indian is gone as far as I'm concerned and I don't want nothing to do with him."

James looked at Jepson, who shifted nervously in his saddle every few seconds. He was a holy man but he looked like he had lost faith in any deity that would protect his soul.

"Now let's go back to town before that bear creature feeds on us next."

"I'm not going back."

"What did you say, son?"

"I'm not going back with you."

"Well, why the hell not?"

James stared into the sheriff's eyes. "Because I have to put a stop to this. I can't explain it right now but I must go after him."

"Boy, you're out of your damned mind. That thing tore men apart. He's going to kill you."

"What does it matter? Carson's mom, George, your men. Nothing can stop him but me."

"George?" Danvers lifted the brim of his hat in disbelief. "He killed George too?"

CURSE OF THE ANCIENTS

"George is alive for now. I don't know if he'll make it though."

Danvers lowered his head, taking in all the information. "If you go after him, son, then you are on your own. I can't help you. We have no way to fight this…this thing. I'm sorry."

James nodded. He had already come to terms with his role in this mess. "I know, sir. I'll be okay." His eyes searched the western horizon. "So you say he's to the west a few miles?"

Sheriff Danvers nodded. He pointed out several markers for James to look out for on the way. He wished James good luck and said he would see to it that James' mother and Carson were looked after. The way he said it led James to believe the sheriff had already written him off as a dead man. His gut told him it would probably be true. Then the men rode off as quickly as they had arrived. Jepson continued to babble aloud as they left.

James felt sick to his stomach. The sheriff was one of the toughest men he knew. Even tougher than George. But he looked broken. James never thought he would ever see the sheriff so vulnerable. So unsure and scared. It rocked him that Danvers and George were defeated by Crouching Bear and yet he had to go forward to face him. Would Crouching Bear listen to James? Would he kill James? Could James really kill him? James had never killed a man before. Now he was faced with killing not only another human being, but a friend.

In all his fantasies of beating bad guys, not once did it involve killing. He imagined shootouts and fist fights. But nobody died. James realized that life was much more real. The stakes were high and it wasn't a game. This manhunt was bigger than the news clippings of his father pistol whipping ruffians. This adventure made his father's exploits seem small. Unimportant. James had embarked on a massive journey, a journey that could tear a man's soul apart. Killing a friend to save the lives of countless folks was epic. Not one choice in the matter was as simple as tossing a drunk out of a saloon. James tried to wrap his mind around this thought.

James spurred his horse to ride westward. He got the horse into a fast gallop since he knew which direction to go. He wouldn't have to worry about searching for footprints or human waste. Time was short if he wanted to catch up with Crouching Bear before more damage could be done. He had to take care of this problem for Carson and George and the rest of the townspeople. But most of all, he had to do it for Crouching Bear. He had to save his friend. To do that, he would have to kill him.

CHAPTER 39

Soaring Eagle removed the bandage that covered George's chest. As he peeled it back, some of the soft scabbing came with it, which elicited a fresh spot of blood. George moaned. The old man applied a new poultice and moved beyond the crushed ribs to the forearm. He gently lifted the arm at the wrist, inspecting the paste that filled in the cavernous wound. He patted the paste down to remove any pockets of air that had crept beneath.

His mind worked hard to find an agreeable excuse for what he had done. But he found no answer. Soaring Eagle wished he could do it all over, knowing then what he knew now.

When James and George had come to him, he had listened to the story of the curse and he had been swept away by it. His intent had been to help the young man eliminate the curse, and free the Indian from his pain. So he offered to assist with the vision quest. Of course, he knew that once the ceremony took place, the two men would be linked forever. He communicated that much to the boy but he had left out one important detail, the fact that one of them would have to die in order for the curse to be lifted. At the time, Soaring Eagle was not connected enough to the boy to worry about events downwind. After meeting with

James again, Soaring Eagle felt more affinity to the youngster. He actually cared about the young man and hoped he would survive this battle. But he knew too well that the events he had set in motion were beyond his control.

What bothered him more was that he now had an affinity for Crouching Bear, as well. When he met the man, he had helped him, as was his nature. Soaring Eagle had always enjoyed helping others which is what led him to learn about the ways of the spirits and the healing practices. Once he heard Crouching Bear's side of the tale, he empathized deeply for the loneliness and pain that the man had portrayed. He was a tragic figure, damned either way he turned. It was heart-breaking.

Soaring Eagle applied a cool compress to George's forehead. The man's fever shot up every few hours as his body fought to survive. He didn't particularly like George but he cared for him anyway. On some level, caring for George was a form of penance for what he had done to James. But mostly, Soaring Eagle would have cared for the injured man regardless of James.

The old man wondered what the spirits had in store for the two men. Each possibility had its benefits and drawbacks. If James killed Crouching Bear, it would forever change the young man. He was innocent and full of life. To kill another man was to chip away at one's soul. If Crouching Bear killed James, the Indian would be free of the curse transforming him into the creature. However, he would still be a man without family and friends, forced to wander the earth in search of meaning. Most likely alone. Most men would prefer death to a sentence of eternal solitude.

Of course, there would be the possibility that both men would die in the struggle. Again, the curse would be banished but two worthy souls would be gone from the earth. A tragedy any way one chose to look at it.

Soaring Eagle sat before the fire and warmed some tea. He grew tired since the vigil came with no breaks. He leaned over the flames to light a reed of incense. To pass some time and take a brief respite, Soaring Eagle would chant to the spirits. His pleas for a swift and humane end to the ordeal would most likely prove fruitless. But he had to try.

George moaned and turned to Soaring Eagle. For the first time, he was struggling to emerge from unconsciousness. His eyes fluttered as he attempted to focus on the old man. "Jaaaames." Hardly a whisper had escaped George's cracked lips. Soaring Eagle heard the faint words and crawled over to his patient. He spoke softly. "Rest. You have some serious injuries."

George fought to keep his eyes open. "Jaaaames."

"James is okay. He went to get help." He lied to George in order to maintain calm. "You just rest and heal. We'll take care of everything else."

George's eyes slammed shut. A long exhale slid from his lips. He had fallen back into unconsciousness. His body had an uphill battle to recover from such damage. Soaring Eagle felt better that George would make it. The simple fact he had awakened so soon showed his spirit was fighting hard. He smiled to himself that George was as much of a warrior on the inside as he was on the outside. He still didn't like him very much.

Soaring Eagle returned to his incense. He closed his eyes and began the rhythmic chant. The ancient Indian language lulled him into a meditative trance. His eyelids fluttered as he sank deeper into the spirit mind. He called out to the gods that traveled to the stars. His cadence reflected a song that transcended time. A prayer passed down, many generations ago, unifying a whole people. It was old. Older than the sands that filled the desserts. Older than the mountains that rose to commune with the gods.

He drifted to the clouds, high above the plains. His third eye opened to the landscape below. He searched for the men, exploring valleys and hills, prairies and forests. The spirits guided him on the journey, shepherding his safe travels. He felt the end was a long way off. Deep in his bones, the truth revealed the need for patience. The floating dissipated as Soaring Eagle returned to the hackle-berry grove, a sound, more persistent and pressing, calling him back to this plane.

Soaring Eagle opened his eyes. George was choking and gasping for air. His body convulsed, racked with pain. The old man hurried to his side and brought a cup of fresh water to George's lips. Most of it trickled down his beard. But some had gotten past his lips, as he felt George swallow with difficulty. Soaring Eagle sighed to himself. All he could do was wait.

CHAPTER 40

Crouching Bear wiped the drool from his mouth. He rolled onto his side and looked around. Gnawed bones with strands of sinew barely attached were scattered in a ten foot radius around his body. It felt like he had swallowed a buffalo. His stomach protruded over his naked manhood. His mouth tasted rotten and he felt a breeze whip through the hole in his cheek.

The Indian sat up and surveyed the killing field, the carnage coming back to him in glimpses. He tried to shake the cobwebs from his mind. He must have fallen asleep in a food-induced coma after devouring the men that had attacked him. The last thing he recalled was chewing on the skull of the red haired man, thinking how human flesh wasn't bad as a food source. Next thing he knew, he had woken up with a distended belly and a foggy head.

Crouching Bear climbed to his feet. His naked skin was darkened by the exposure to the afternoon sun. He made his way to the clothes he had taken from George. They were still piled in the grass at the top of the bank. He walked slowly, the discomfort in his belly sloshing around.

Crouching Bear knew James was coming. He could feel the certainty throughout his being. It was not something he looked forward to. He wanted to keep running until James gave up, but he also knew that wouldn't happen. Better to face the situation and have the spirits settle it once and for all. Even if it meant he killed his friend.

The pressure in his stomach forced him to break wind. The relief was immediate but he would have to move his bowels before he could feel more normal. He settled into a notch of the stream's bank. The natural cutout gave him room to rest his hands so he could eliminate with some comfort and ease.

Crouching Bear discovered a change in his perception. He had decided to fight this curse to the bitter end. No longer would he waste time worrying about James. The boy was hunting him down so he would punish James for it. He embraced the bear nature, the animal brain that provided so much power. He accepted the fate of the spirits. His warrior soul was doomed for eternity anyway. So he would go out with a fight.

His determination gave him courage and strength. He realized his weakness had been feeling sorry for James and Carson. Being ashamed of what he had done to Minnie and the others. But he was just doing what a bear would. He was living. Tucked in the back of his mind, of course, he still regretted what had happened. He liked his new friends and wished things could be different, that circumstances would allow them to be together as friends forever. It just hadn't worked out that way. He wouldn't surrender. He intended to live or die trying. There was more comfort in knowing and being certain as opposed to fearing and hoping.

Crouching Bear finished relieving himself of the digested remains, the acrid odor more pleasant somehow. It tickled a primal sense of smell within his brain. So many changes, he thought to himself. It would be exciting to learn what his new form was capable of. To push the limits and explore the unknown. It was a challenge worth accepting.

As he pulled on the dungarees, Crouching Bear wrestled with his next move. Should he wait for James to find him while preparing for the fight? Should he chase down James and bring the fight to him? Catch him off guard? An unexpected move which could certainly swing the odds in his favor. The element of surprise is what his tribe (former tribe, he chided himself) would use when attacking a settlement or travelers. Hitting an enemy when they weren't expecting you allowed you to take advantage of their lack of preparation. The idea intrigued him and he felt he was leaning toward that option.

He lifted the leather jacket and began to put it on when he changed his mind. He tossed it on the ground and felt proud to reject the clothing. What purpose did he have wearing a white man's jacket? And what did he need pants for? Crouching Bear sloughed off the dungarees and stood naked. His mind gathered power from the mammalian side. He would fight James as the bear so there would be no need of clothing, especially white man clothing. Bears stayed warm because of their fur. Their skin was protected by their fur. Crouching Bear would become one with the spirit of the bear. He would use all the tools the bear provided him for survival. He felt much stronger and larger with his new-found pride.

The Indian climbed up the bank and surveyed the landscape to his east. It might be a short journey if he met James on the trail. The time to fight was now. His power was at its fullest now. He would be victorious and revel in the glory of the beast. He would taste the blood of his enemies. He would devour all human flesh that made the mistake of coming between him and his future.

Crouching Bear sucked in the air, almost hyper-ventilating with excited anticipation. He screamed as loud as he could, summoning the animal, from his diaphragm. He was a warrior spirit again. The bear was a warrior. He charged up the hill, naked against the sun and wind. The rage warred in his heart. James was no longer his friend, but an enemy to be crushed under heel. Crouching Bear roared and ran. The long grass whipped his legs. Birds fled to the skies. The horizon rushed at him as he sped along the trail to James. He would bring the fight to him today.

CHAPTER 41

He had made up his mind. He would kill Crouching Bear. He had to. It was the best option. James hated himself for arriving at this conclusion but what choice did he have?

James cried as he rode. He had tried to stop the tears, admonishing himself for being a baby. But he eventually let it go. His emotions were too strong. In a few short days, he had had to completely grow up from a teenager thinking he was a man. Loved ones had died. Friends had been maimed. And now he had to kill a man. A friend.

The horse galloped over the hilly plains, avoiding rocks and ravines. The saddle shifted from side to side since James had not re-tightened the billet straps before leaving Soaring Eagle's den. He used his inner thighs to clamp on to the horse's back as tight as he could.

Thoughts of Carson flooded his mind. He missed his best friend so much. After years of growing up together, he had become accustomed to eating meals together and sharing dreams of exciting futures. James snickered as he thought how he hated to play cards with Carson. The boy always told him he wasn't paying attention but it was absurd. He watched the kid shuffle and deal the cards. He studied his own cards and even tried to figure out how Carson always ended up with a winning hand.

What he missed most about Carson was his happiness. Carson was always happy. He enjoyed every moment of life. When people made fun of him or treated him like dirt because he was slow, Carson kept on smiling. Maybe he didn't always understand that people were being cruel to him. But sometimes he did. And his smile would fade but he would turn it around somehow. He would ask the lady if she needed help with her groceries. Or he would volunteer to work for Filler without pay. He just wanted to be a part of things. To be loved and wanted. Such a great kid. God had blessed him with being the best person in the world, even though he was not a regular kid.

James recalled overhearing his mother talking to Minnie one day. It was about five or six years ago. Minnie had told his mother that she hoped he would live long enough to become a man. Apparently, children with his condition didn't live long lives. James had run off to the hiding spot by himself and cried for hours. The thought of losing his little "brother" had smashed his heart. And that was really before Carson was old enough to show the type of person he was today. When he had gone home, James had asked his mother about the conversation and he wept uncontrollably in front of her. When he looked up, his mother was crying too. She held James close for a long time and told him that God would always look out for Carson and that we needed to help God by taking care of the boy too.

Fresh tears rolled down James' cheeks. Life could be harsh. Cruel. Poor Carson had a difficult life already with his childish mind. Now he would have to grow up without a mother. How many times can a small boy be kicked before he stops getting up? Why did the nice people seem to suffer the most? He recalled his mother once telling him that only the good people died young. He hoped that was wrong for Carson's sake. Although, if it were true, men like Filler and Wilson would probably live to be two hundred years old.

He shook his head to rid himself of his sad thoughts. He had to focus on the task at hand. He had to shift his mind to become harder. More calloused. The monumental feat before him required him to be something he was not. He was a good person. His mother had raised him to be good and respectful. He hardly ever had thoughts of hurting another person. Sure, when Filler was extra surly, he would daydream of punching that crooked nose. And when he got fed up with cleaning all of George's spitting misses, he imagined himself whacking the large man across the head with the broom handle. But James had never been in a fight or had reason to hurt a person until these last few days. And now he had to go from a non-violent life to killing a human being. It was a huge leap and he knew he had to become something tougher and less thoughtful.

James spurred the horse to pick up the pace. As he re-focused his mind on the fight with Crouching Bear, his energy levels rose. His sense of purpose solidified. James wanted to find Crouching Bear and end the curse quickly. Before anyone else got hurt. And before he softened up again.

He tried to envision how the encounter would go. Would he just sneak up on Crouching Bear and attack him? Would that even be possible? The Indian had grown up in the wilderness and James didn't think he could sneak up on someone who was always attuned to self-preservation in the elements. Or would Crouching Bear attack him? Maybe he should slow down in case he crested a hill and found Crouching Bear in his animal form, poised to eat him whole. Would the two men exchange words before the battle? Like an old story about the knights in shining armor. The knights would usually state their claims to such and such kingdom or to avenging the death of their father. The men would then proceed to lance each other from horseback or charge on foot with iron swords smelted in the fires of a famous blacksmith. James snorted that this would not go quite so romantically like a storybook tale.

James pictured Crouching Bear attacking George, sinking his sharp jaws into his friend's arm. He saw the blood spurts. He heard the screams of agony. He felt the rage of the beast and the horror of the scene. It emboldened him. His time to become a man was now. He had to face down his primal fears. He must become a monster to defeat one.

CHAPTER 42

Sheriff Danvers rode into town with Jepson at his side. Both men were exhausted and defeated. They rode in silence the whole way back to town, only exchanging glances of disbelief and shattered souls.

As the men came down the street, Wilson, drunk, as usual, even at this fine hour of the afternoon, pointed and shouted that the men had returned. The folks that were bustling in town dropped what they were doing to approach the sheriff and his solo posse. A few store windows were open, and folks rushed out into the street upon hearing Wilson's slurred shouts.

The crowd circled the riders so they could ride no further. Jepson slid off his saddle and dropped to the dirt in tears. He cried out that it was so horrible and blood was everywhere and the Indian was a monster straight out of hell. Women gasped and children hid their faces in the skirts of their mothers. Some of the men were shouting over the noise to find out what had happened and where the other men were. Jepson carried on without responding to any of it. He was broken. Danvers knew the Doc would have to give him some tinctures to calm the hysteria.

Sheriff Danvers held up a shaky hand to quiet the crowd. He had wanted to take time to prepare words for the public. He didn't want to frighten people or send the town into a panic. But his mind was a mess the whole ride back. He couldn't focus on words. Only getting back to town. And trying to rid his mind of the gory scenes. Alas, it was useless.

"Folks. Please. Please. Calm down." He thought to himself that he was telling the people to be calm when his body quivered in fear.

Wilson, the drunken mouthpiece of the common man, stumbled to the inner circle. "Ain'tcha gonna show us the scalp'n all of that danged Injun?"

"Shut up, Wilson." Danvers had no patience for Wilson's crap today. He controlled his temper to keep from jumping down and cold cocking the idiot right across the jaw. "The search is over. It is time for us to return to regular town life."

The crowd all spoke over each other, questioning what the hell that meant, where was Hannigan, did they kill that damned red man, how come only two of you returned, what should they tell their families? Danvers closed his eyes to try to shut out the angry mob.

"Quiet." He shouted over their heads. The crowd slowly stopped yelling. The murmur lowered to a few whispers but mostly silence. The faces stared at him, wanting information. Needing the truth. He sighed as he knew he would have to be frank with them. He had always called it like he saw it and they expected him to be that way, regardless of the news. So nothing should change now; although, this situation was far worse than a simple bank-robbing or a cattle theft.

"They're dead." The faces sank in shock. Nobody said a word. "Hannigan, Murphy, Thomas. All dead."

Mayor Cosby waddled to the front with his hands on his hips. "Whaddaya mean they're dead?"

"They're dead. Just like I told you. It was awful. The Indian was...was...a bear. Some sort of bear."

The mayor looked at the faces to his left and then his right. "Whaddaya mean he was a bear? Are you saying that a bear killed our men?"

"Yes. Well, no. Sort of. The Indian turned into a bear. Right in front of our eyes." Jepson wailed again as he beat the dirt below his hands. He hadn't gotten off his hands and knees since he had slid off his horse.

"I've never seen anything like it before in my life. We had him surrounded. He was right there within reach. And then, he was a bear."

The crowd exchanged incredulous looks and patted their hands and sobbed.

"It killed the men and we high-tailed it out of there as fast as we could. I'm telling you bullets did no good there. We were overwhelmed." He paused and scratched his beard. He lifted the brim of his hat, no longer able to hide the tears that streamed down his face.

The mayor and the townspeople stood silent. They were all in shock at what he was telling them. He knew they didn't believe him. Hell, he didn't believe his own words. But it was all he had. The images replayed in his mind over and over again.

Mayor Cosby wrung his hands. "Well we gotta go get some blood for blood. I want every man and able-bodied shooter to get saddled up so we can go kill that sumbitch."

"Nobody is going anywhere or I will shoot them where they stand." The crowd gasped again. The mayor looked angry and his hands went right back to his hips. Before he could respond, Danvers spoke further. "There ain't no amount of men or guns that could bring this thing down. I'm telling you. You know those men were the toughest of the tough. We went with guns on our sides and revenge in our hearts and we were whipped. That beast is supernatural." He choked on his words. "It is straight out of hell."

Nobody said a word.

"If you go after that thing, then mark my words, you will end up like the others. We are best off going about our regular lives and staying right here in our town. Ain't nothing beyond those hills but evil."

Filler stood in the back of the crowd, holding a mug and his dish rag. "What about George? I heard the bastard ran off with James just like you boys did. They dead, too?"

The sheriff shook his head. "No. At least James is still alive. George is hurt real bad. Ain't sure he'll pull through. Gotta wait and see."

"Where is my son?" Sarah Johnson came through the crowd. Her eyes were full of tears and she dabbed at her face with her handkerchief. "Where is James?"

"He kept going. On his own." The crowd gasped in disbelief again. Sarah stepped forward with pain on her face. "I tried to talk him out of it, ma'am. But he insisted he see it through. Nothing I could have done unless I beat him with a stick." Sarah dropped at the news and a few men helped her back to her feet.

"The only thing we can do now, the best thing we can do, is pray for that boy. Pray that the hand of God protects him. Pray that George pulls through." Wilson snorted at that comment. He obviously had little regard for the big man who tossed him into the street almost nightly. "This here is the work of the devil. And only God above can send it back to hell."

CHAPTER 43

James tugged the reins hard. The horse obeyed and stopped immediately. He squinted across the fields to validate what he thought he saw. A figure was running toward him several hundred yards ahead. He struggled to identify the man. James thought it might be Crouching Bear. But something didn't appear right. The man was definitely Indian as his skin was darkened and his long black hair flowed in the wind behind him.

James' stomach flipped inside. The nerves of a coming fight swirled through his intestines and caused some bile to creep up his throat. He swallowed hard and stared ahead at the man coming his way. It looked like it could be Crouching Bear but he was…naked. James leaned back, not believing his eyes. He had half expected to see Crouching Bear in George's clothing since his garments were missing when they had regained consciousness. He also figured that Crouching Bear might be wearing some of the clothes worn by the posse if he had ripped through the fibers again. He never expected to see Crouching Bear naked. Not now. Not at any time. It was so bizarre James was frightened.

The raging Indian was screaming as he ran across the wind-swept grass. The sounds were distant but getting louder as he neared. James' horse whinnied as it sensed something dangerous. Perhaps evil, James questioned. He rubbed its neck and shushed the horse to calm its fears. He thought, to himself, he wished someone were rubbing him and ridding his own fears. Because he was scared. Very scared.

James watched his friend approaching fast. He slid out of the saddle and pulled the handgun from the back of his pants. He raised the pistol at his friend and closed his left eye to aim through the sights. The Indian was still out of range of the gun but James wanted to try to scare Crouching Bear. It didn't seem to work as the man kept running and screaming. James noticed his gun hand shaking and he tried to will it to steady, but his limbs ignored his brain.

He checked the chamber and found it filled with six shots. James walked over to his saddle bag and dug out a handful of new bullets. He dumped the shells in his back pocket which was wider for his hand to slide in than the smaller pockets on the front of his dungarees. He sighted in the pistol again, closing his left eye and staring down the barrel. Crouching Bear kept coming hard and was close to being in range. James hesitated. He intended originally to fire a warning shot so Crouching Bear would stop. Then he would try to talk to his friend before killing him. He wanted his friend to know he had liked him and was sorry for having to kill him. It wasn't a revenge kill but rather a kill to save Crouching Bear from a life of pain and hurting others. Then James changed his mind and decided to fire a shot at Crouching Bear as soon as he could. If he could put the man down with a shot from a distance, he could control the battle and do things on his terms. Now he changed his mind again. James thought he should just fire the warning shot and hope that plan worked.

James cocked the hammer back and steadied his hand as much as he could. He slowly squeezed the trigger, afraid of the loud bang and the recoil of the weapon. But he broke the trigger past the point of no return and the gun shot was off. The recoil wasn't as bad as James had anticipated. However, the sound of the gun shot was much louder than James had counted on. His ears rang loudly, drowning out the screams of his friend.

The bullet skittered across the dirt before the Indian's feet and a hair to the left. Crouching Bear ran without pausing. The shot hadn't affected his disposition in the slightest. James swallowed hard again.

What could he do next? Should he fire again? Should he shield himself behind his horse? Maybe he should jump back on the horse and ride just far enough to stay outside of Crouching Bear's reach. He might tire the man down if he provoked the Indian to chase him all around. Crouching Bear was closing fast. James had to make a move now. He was out of time.

James raised the gun again. This time his hand was steady. Full of conviction. He re-cocked the hammer. He closed his left eye and sighted in the target. "I will shoot you." He yelled to his friend, who either didn't hear James' threat over his own screaming or he had chosen to ignore James. Either way, James figured he had warned him. Fair and square. This would be on Crouching Bear.

He pulled the trigger and the bullet punctured through Crouching Bear's right shoulder. Blood sprayed behind the naked man as the bullet passed straight through. The hit stunned James' friend but only for a brief moment. He continued to run at James. Before James could fire another shot, Crouching Bear slammed into him with all his might. Crouching Bear was bigger than James to begin with. Adding the Indian's speed at a full sprint, the force of the men colliding was like a train barreling through a brick wall.

James flew backward with the air leaving his lungs. He landed hard on the dry earth and Crouching Bear's momentum carried him several yards beyond where James lie. Crouching Bear rolled over and sprung to his feet. James sat up, choking to get oxygen into his body. He had managed to hold onto the pistol and he raised it at his friend. James felt like one of his lungs had collapsed. Or, at least, he imagined that this must be what it would feel like.

Crouching Bear stood in front of James with blood dripping from the wound in his shoulder. His eyes glared with a red shine. The naked man's muscles flexed and rippled as he poised for another attack. His skin started to change. Crouching Bear lifted his head to the sky and howled, a deep guttural howl that was more animal than human. Froth filled the corners of his lips. James looked on in horror.

CHAPTER 44

Crouching Bear felt the changes consuming him. He recognized the signs now, when the transformation was about to take hold. His blood would boil within his veins. The burn would quickly turn into an itching sensation, as if millions of insects crawled within the vessels of his body. Yet he knew he couldn't scratch the itch or get at them. He felt his skin warm and stretch. It moved, on its own, to accommodate the shifting bones. It was terrible the first time it had happened. But each successive instance had become more welcome. A part of him. A natural cleansing almost.

He roared at the spirits above and looked at his bullet wound. The hole in his shoulder sizzled and shrunk as the fur and skin swallowed up the absence of flesh. His mouth and nose protruded into a muzzle, a snout dripping with saliva. Crouching Bear fell to his knees and his back arched toward the sun. The splintering crunch of his spine stretched his torso to twice its length, the hands and feet bloating with cartilage, becoming pads and paws. His nails turned blacker than night and thinned, growing inches beyond the fur. Skin rippled as it moved to allow room for denser bones and thicker musculature. Dark fur bristled through tiny pores, causing the Indian agony as they sprung through and then drooped under their own weight.

James' horse whinnied and ran off.

Crouching Bear felt more than a man. He was awesome. Powerful. Fully realized. His mind had willed the change to overtake him almost as much as the anger had helped it along. He had more control of the beast. Its mind was his mind. Its desires were his desires. Its survival, his survival.

Standing on his hind legs, Crouching Bear reached over eight feet in height. His perspective on the ground below chilled him. He imagined the hawk that drifted high above the canyons with such a mighty view. His mind realized that he preferred the beast instead of the man. Man was so limited but the animal was free. It had only nourishment, shelter and survival. Nothing more. No elders to answer to. No woman to control his manly desires. No children to burden his movements. Just the beast and whatever the beast wanted.

He howled again and again. He watched James cowering in the dirt like the weak being he was. The fight was over before it had started. Crouching Bear felt his blood surge through his veins with rage and the expectation of victory. He dropped down to all fours and stepped in the direction of his old friend. James spoke but he ignored the words. Time of talk had passed like the evening stars. There was nothing James could say to save his life now.

Crouching Bear lunged at James and swiped his massive claws across the gun barrel. The pistol flew in the air. James crawled backwards on his rear to escape the bear. He wasn't about to let the boy escape. He flung himself at James and landed on his legs. James shrieked and kicked as hard as he could. The shin bones slammed into Crouching Bear's stomach without damage. Crouching Bear thought to himself how he hardly even felt the kicks against his beefy mid-section.

He leaned down to tear a hunk of James' stomach away. James twisted just enough that the bear's jaw only clasped dungarees and some shirt tail. The button to the dungarees popped off in Crouching Bear's mouth. He let it fall to the dirt before accidentally swallowing it. It angered him that James evaded his bite. Crouching Bear raised his furry arm and drove the claws into the left bicep of his old friend. James screamed as he tried to crawl out from under him on his side. Now he had James pinned to the ground through his arm. Blood squirted into Crouching Bear's face, spray reaching his tongue. It tasted salty and warm and it made him hungry for more.

James squirmed under the claws as they buried deeper into his flesh. Each time he wriggled more skin tore away and blood flowed. The boy swung his other arm into the snout of Crouching Bear. The force of the punch stunned him and he thought to himself that he had definitely felt the blow. It angered him more and he snapped his jaws at the retreating fist. The teeth clicked together as the bite missed. Crouching Bear ducked his head to try to bite James' stomach. He wanted to eviscerate the boy and thrash his innards across the field. His downward motion was thwarted as James brought a rock into his mouth. The stone broke a few of his front teeth off, a couple falling to the ground, and one got swallowed as he sucked in air.

Crouching Bear stood on his hind legs in visceral reaction to the broken teeth. It hurt badly to have the nerves inside the teeth exposed to the elements. He bellowed in anguish. He was almost beside himself at how the events were unfolding. His initial impression was a swift and easy defeat over James. Yet he kept encountering setbacks and counter-moves. His mind became a jumble of confusion, rage and self-doubt. Had he underestimated James? Did James possess a talisman of some sort that was protecting him from the attack? He couldn't help but think back to the curse. Perhaps the curse was more than he had figured. Maybe there was no way to win and bury the curse along with his tormentors.

Crouching Bear roared once more and fixed his gaze upon James. James had gotten to his feet and was frantically searching for the handgun. He clutched at his wounds, applying pressure to the four bloody holes in his arm. His eyes grew wide as he looked for the pistol. Watching James' reaction renewed Crouching Bear's confidence. He knew he still had the upper hand. He had to strike while James was scared and wounded. And it helped that he no longer had the gun in his hands.

Crouching Bear growled and charged James again.

CHAPTER 45

J ames watched in horror. Even though it was the second time he had seen the transformation, it was no easier to accept. Crouching Bear screamed as the bullet wound on his shoulder smoked and then shrank. James couldn't believe the hole almost sealed up with no ointments or bandages.

He winced when the loud crack of bone popping sounded. Crouching Bear's skin stretched and shifted outward to allow room for his bones to grow into those of the bear. Fur squiggled out of his skin and quickly covered his misshapen body. His hands and feet had turned into paws with long black nails. James worried more about the claws than anything else. Those claws could do a lot of damage to a man before the sharp teeth even got close to him.

The whole transformation took only seconds. Crouching Bear screamed and howled throughout the process. James' horse didn't stick around to see the finish. He watched the horse run off quickly. James watched the bear stand on its hind legs and bellow at the sky. He was mesmerized by the enormous size of the animal. It had to be over eight feet tall if it was an inch.

Crouching Bear kept howling, staring down at James. He knew he had to move but he was practically paralyzed with fear. The confidence and determination escaped James as he wet himself. If he weren't scared out of his mind, he would have chastised himself for displaying such a sign of immaturity.

James shook the fog from his brain and raised the pistol at his friend. As he tried to cock the hammer, Crouching Bear lunged at him and swung his massive paw at James. The paw connected with the barrel of the gun and sent the weapon flying. Surprised by the blow, James scrambled like a crab on his backside. He had to get away as fast as he could.

The bear jumped on James' legs. The sheer weight of the animal forced a scream out of him. He kicked his legs up and down to hurt Crouching Bear. Instead, his legs bounced off the soft belly of the beast with ineffectual results. James struggled with how to escape. The bear was much too big and very fast. He was in a panic to figure things out while fending off the beast.

Crouching Bear thrust his muzzle at James' stomach. James tried to roll on his side to protect as much of his organs as possible. The bear chomped down, tearing away a section of his pants. It nearly missed disemboweling him.

Then his friend dug his claws into James' bicep, pinning the arm to the earth. James screamed so hard his throat got sore. He felt each individual claw, four of them, wriggling through his muscles; the warmth of his blood leaking down his arm. Some of James' blood had squirted into Crouching Bear's muzzle. Red droplets decorated the furry snout. James tried to wrestle his arm free but each time he moved the claws tore away more flesh, making the wounds bigger.

In a last ditch effort to survive, James swung his right arm at the bear's face. His punch connected with the large nose. James thought he recognized stun in his friend's eyes. So he punched again. Crouching Bear tried to bite his fist but missed, the sound of his teeth crashing together like a loud snap. James realized, momentarily, he was no longer afraid. But he had to fight hard to survive. His hand bumped a large rock on the ground. James snatched it up and swung it around into the mouth of the animal. The timing saved James as Crouching Bear was trying once again to bite into his stomach. A few broken teeth bounced onto James' chest.

The strike definitely hurt Crouching Bear because he stood back up and roared at the sun. The sound was a mixture of anger and pain. James got excited for a moment that he might have a chance to defeat Crouching Bear. It would be a small chance, but he would take anything at this moment.

He took advantage of Crouching Bear's anguish and climbed to his feet. He had to find his gun but he had no idea where it had landed. He didn't pay attention to its trajectory because he was focused on avoiding the attack. His left bicep throbbed. As he frantically searched for his weapon, he clasped his bleeding wounds to stem the flow. The holes burned like he was a cattle getting branded. A brief thought flashed across his mind that he was glad he wasn't a steer.

James searched desperately. He spun in a circle, his eyes wide. Searching. Looking. Nothing. His mind began to play images of his imminent death. He saw Crouching Bear stomping his body into the dirt, then gnawing on his bloody limbs. Carson was crying, walking aimlessly in a dense forest. Calling out his name. Lonely for his friend. The bear sucking the marrow from his bones. A long pink tongue lapping up the fragments that stuck to its lips. Carrion circled high above him as they awaited their turn at his dinner table. Crouching Bear sharing his meat with Carson because he was angry at James for introducing the Indian to his momma and then leaving Carson all alone in the world.

The images played over and over. His search for the gun was proving fruitless. A flutter in his gut told him he had to snap out of this reverie. He was in mortal danger and he had to act fast. There would be plenty of time to reflect on his mistakes as the bear consumed his flesh.

James gave up looking for the pistol. It was probably close by but, with everything going on, he was sure he was overlooking its blatant location. He squeezed his arm tighter as he noticed the flow of blood soaking his shirt sleeve. All he could hope for was a chance to kill the bear. His horse was gone. The gun was lost. And he was quickly running out of strength and blood. James turned on his heels to face Crouching Bear. All the while the creature howled and roared but the hairs on the back of James' neck pricked up.

He stared his friend down.

Crouching Bear growled and charged James again.

CHAPTER 46

James saw him coming. Clutching his arm, he spun at the last second and the bear went rushing by him. He turned at the same time as his friend. His mind screamed that he wished he didn't have to fight his friend. A voice returned the thought in his head. *It is too late for wishes.*

James' blood ran cold. Who was that voice from? It wasn't his, he was damned sure of that. It didn't even sound like his voice. It sounded more like…Crouching Bear? But how?

We are one. The curse bond has brought us together. But the bond must be broken.

Crouching Bear stared at James with red eyes. His back and shoulders rose and fell with labored breaths. James found himself speechless, for a moment, as he watched his friend.

"You can't do this, Crouching Bear. You have to give up."

It is you who must give up. I am more powerful. I am in control.

James heard the voice in his head but the bear kept panting. Watching.

"I don't want to kill you but I have no choice. You have hurt too many people."

One more might be better. And you are a tasty one, James.

James grimaced at the thought-voice. He felt like his friend was toying with him. It made him angry that Crouching Bear was gone, locked away deep inside all that fur.

"You could have turned yourself in. You could have come with me. Instead you killed more people."

I am surviving. Your town would have me killed. My own people would have me killed. So I decided to stand and fight.

"It didn't have to end this way. Look what you have done. Your spirits will never accept you into their realm now."

The spirits turned their back on me the moment I was cursed. I could never earn back my place in the heavens.

James glanced down at his arm. His shirt sleeve was covered in dark blood. His arm kept throbbing. He hoped he could use the arm to defend himself.

You could use eight arms, James. You still wouldn't defeat me.

He forgot Crouching Bear could hear his thoughts. How was he going to kill the Indian if he knew his moves before James made them? Not only was the bear bigger and stronger than James but it could also read his mind. He was trapped.

The thought-voice laughed in his head. Crouching Bear was enjoying this. He was playing with his food. The thought-voice laughed again. This time more heartily. James stared at the glowing red eyes. Drool dripped in long, slow globs. The beast salivated at the meal before it.

"What happened to you? The man I knew was good. Friendly. You're just a monster now."

A monster YOU created, James. I, alone, was cursed until you got involved. You extended the reach of the curse when you went on the vision quest. That blood covers your hands as much as it does mine.

"No. No, I didn't slaughter those people. You did. You would have done it whether we connected or not. You know that's the truth. You allowed the evil to take over."

Evil is everywhere, James. The white man is evil toward the red man. Toward the black man. And the creatures. You have no right to judge.

"I can't be held responsible for what others have done. We all have responsibility for our own actions. You can't blame what happened to you on anyone else. You killed your warrior brother. That's what started it all."

It was an accident. I never meant to hurt my own people.

The thought-voice shouted in James' head. He knew he had touched a raw nerve.

"It doesn't erase what happened. You killed him and that is all that matters. And, because of your accident, more people have died. What did Minnie or George or those men in the posse have to do with you killing your tribesman?"

The bear growled. Its front paws scratched the dirt as it shifted its stance.

All of that is in the past. What matters now is killing you, James. You are trying to stop me. You are chasing me across the lands. I will not rest until you are gone.

"That's funny because I won't rest until YOU are gone."

Crouching Bear appeared to be losing patience with James. He growled again and more slop dripped from his muzzle. The red eyes flared brighter.

You will have to pay for what you have done to me. After I kill you, I will hunt down your mother and your little friend, Carson. They shall suffer because of you.

James let go of his injured arm. He stepped toward Crouching Bear, no longer afraid. He was furious. James was willing to sacrifice himself but he couldn't allow harm to come to the people he loved the most. "What did you say?"

You heard what I said. I am going to devour you. And then I am going to feast on your lovely mother. And the little slow one.

James was beside himself. It was all he could do to keep from rushing at Crouching Bear. What had become of his friend? The townspeople called Indians savages. Crouching Bear was behaving like a savage. Although, James knew the bear spirit was dominating the man. James took a few more steps toward Crouching Bear. He was close enough he could smell the musk of the animal. He couldn't have been further than four feet from the beast.

Oh, don't get upset, James. The most merciful thing for Carson would be his death. He is useless to anyone and a burden on his caretakers. Besides, you can be together again in death.

James screamed. The rage pumped through his body. Any pain from the claw marks disappeared. Fear of death or being eaten alive faded. He saw red, pure aggression and violence. James had never gotten this mad before. His extremities shook. His knees buckled. He felt dizzy. He tasted blood lust.

James threw himself at Crouching Bear. The battle was on.

CHAPTER 47

When James ran at Crouching Bear, the animal began to raise itself up on its hind legs. James filled his fists with tufts of dark fur. He wrenched the bear's shoulders to the right in an attempt to knock it off balance. His plan didn't work but the bear showed signs of being stunned. Its reactions were delayed, indicating James had caught it off guard.

James drove his legs forward so hard that his face smashed into Crouching Bear's chest. He opened his mouth wide and bit flabby meat through the dense patch of fur. Crouching Bear shrieked and clawed at James' back. The nails sliced through James' back and dug trenches of bloody scratches. The pain just made James gnash his teeth harder. He shook his head left and right, tearing the bear's skin. His mouth filled with the coppery taste of blood. He started to gag from all the hair.

Crouching Bear pawed James' head and threw him off forcefully. James landed on his wounded arm. Waves of pain shot up to his shoulder. He felt something hard under his hip. His hands traced the outline of a pistol. He grabbed it by the barrel just before Crouching Bear reached him. James raised his arm to fend off the monster's bite. He shoved his forearm into the bear's open jaws. Crouching Bear chomped down as he tried to pin James to the ground. James screamed as the teeth sank into his skin.

He swung the gun across the head of the bear, stunning it. He repeated the pistol whipping. Crouching Bear wobbled, dazed from the strikes. His jaw didn't release James' forearm though. He swung the pistol a third time but the bear slammed its paw down on James' arm. With both arms restrained, James found himself in a jam. He needed to get out from under Crouching Bear but the creature was too big. Its weight was enormous. James wrenched his arm, trying to free it from the bear's mouth. It only caused more pain. The bear's jaws were much too powerful for him to free his arm. With no options left, James lowered his arm closer to his face. The bear's head moved closer as it held his arm in its teeth.

James threw his forehead forward. It smashed Crouching Bear's snout with a deafening crunch. Blood poured out of the nostrils right into James' mouth. Crouching Bear squealed and released the arm from his jaws. Instinctively, the bear brought both paws to its nose as the pain pierced its brain. James spun the pistol around in his left hand and squeezed the trigger. A loud report echoed over the fields. The bullet penetrated the bear's stomach with a spray of blood.

Crouching Bear fell over, clutching at his belly. The point blank shot caused a lot of damage. The bear was wounded badly. James didn't want to waste time while he had the beast down. He jumped to his feet and approached the bear with the gun held out. As he neared the writhing animal, James stopped in his tracks. The pained wails of the beast upset James. He had never killed in anger or revenge before. He pitied his friend. James suffered internally for hurting someone he cared about, even though he understood the necessity of it.

Do it. Finish me. You win, James. Do it now.

James' eyes filled with tears. He felt sorry for Crouching Bear. James regretted getting involved with his friend, and the events which followed. He fired another round. This shot penetrated the bear's chest. A plume of blood shot into the air. Droplets of bright red blood tipped the coarse dark fur. James felt the hot tears running down his face.

It is okay, James. You had to do it. Do not worry about me.

The huge beast lie sprawled on the grass. A pool of blood stretched out beneath it. The pink tongue started to hang outside its jaws in a pathetic display. The glowing red eyes returned to a dark brown hue. They appeared to shrink in size too. James cried, gun still pointed at the bear.

As James stared at his dying friend, Crouching Bear began to transform back into human form. The fur disintegrated. Claws retracted and bones shifted. His skin returned to a reddish brown without hair. James saw the bullet wounds which leaked vast amounts of blood. One was square in the middle of Crouching Bear's abdomen. The other was inches from his heart, near the center of his chest. James stepped closer and lowered his gun.

Tell Carson I am sorry. I never meant to hurt him.

James cried harder at Crouching Bear's apology. His thoughts ran back to his little friend. He was happy he would see him again. But saddened with how he had to return to town. Crouching Bear was choking on blood. His teeth were red and James couldn't tell how much of it was his own. He placed the gun on the ground and lie down next to Crouching Bear. James held his friend in his arms, listening to the wheezing from the hole in his chest. James squeezed his friend to his body.

"I'm so sorry, Crouching Bear. You are still my friend. Please forgive me."

Crouching Bear couldn't respond. The gurgling blood in his throat prevented him from talking. James could feel the life fading out of his friend's body. He reached down and unsheathed his knife. He grasped the handle tightly and then stuck it into Crouching Bear's heart. "I'm sorry." James whispered into his dead friend's ear. A sigh of air escaped Crouching Bear as he went limp. His eyes stared up at the heavens. A place his spirit warrior could not go. A single tear slid from one of his eyes.

James stayed with Crouching Bear for a long time. He cried and wished he had never been in this position. He didn't want to leave because that would mean he wouldn't see Crouching Bear anymore. James wept and prayed his friend's soul would be welcomed into white man heaven. That way he could see his friend again in the afterlife.

CHAPTER 48

James walked right into the hackle-berry grove. He was so tired he didn't even bother signaling to Soaring Eagle that he was coming in. Part of him hoped the old man would jump out and finish him off. James regretted killing Crouching Bear and felt like he deserved to be killed himself.

Soaring Eagle must have known it was James coming because he sat comfortably next to the fire. He wore a smile as a greeting to the weary traveler. James nodded imperceptibly, afraid his head would roll off his neck if he exerted himself too much. James dropped to the floor and stared up at the opening above. He could make out the faint glow of a few stars.

"You have returned."

James didn't answer right away. He was still so sad and tried to gather his thoughts without breaking into tears. A man didn't cry, especially in front of other men. And he knew he was a man now that he had undertaken such a huge responsibility. Killing a friend was not something a boy could do.

"Your friend has returned." Soaring Eagle spoke to George. James realized who he was speaking to and he sprung up on all fours. James saw George reclined on the other side of the fire. His eyes were open but he still looked so weak, his cheeks sunken.

"George. How are you doing?" James felt re-energized immediately upon finding his friend to be living.

George nodded. He spat from his reclined position but most of the juice landed on his bandaged chest. James laughed and slapped the dirt.

"I am not cleaning that up, man."

George smiled. Soaring Eagle laughed too. He explained to James that George had come around slowly. Apparently the only two things he had said since awakening were how is James and can you get me my tobacco. They both laughed at George who just kept smiling. He was too weak to speak or laugh at himself. But it appeared he understood the humor in the men's ribbing.

Soaring Eagle made tea and a strange broth to give James back some energy. He worked on James' wounds, chastising him for his shoddy first aid skills. James ate and drank as Soaring Eagle applied ointments and herbal medicines to the scratches on his back and the holes in his bicep.

James told the men the story of how he had encountered the defeated posse and had chosen to go on alone. He recounted the epic battle with the evil beast. He cried as he related the details of his friend's death. James knew real men didn't cry but his emotions were too strong to contain. He gave in and let it out. Both Soaring Eagle and George respectfully diverted their eyes to allow James some dignity while he cried. Neither man commented on the emotions.

When he had finished getting the men up to speed, James sighed and sat back. He stared at the flames as they danced and crackled along the wood. The silence filled the air. It was comforting to James to be able to sit in silence and lose himself in the fire light. George closed his eyes to get more rest. Soaring Eagle busied himself with kindling and preparing more medicinal bandages.

James closed his own eyes. The exhaustion settled in his bones. He felt aches and pains all over his body. The scratches on his back burned. His head throbbed endlessly from smashing Crouching Bear's nose. His mind replayed the battle and the aftermath, each image stirring different emotions, which crested and plunged in James heart. He already missed Crouching Bear.

His thoughts started to return to his mother and Carson. He wondered how his mother was doing. He knew she was probably very worried about him. She was a great mother. Sometimes over-protective, but she did everything for James. She worked so hard to take care of him. But now that he was a man, he wanted to switch things around. He wanted to provide for his mother so that she wouldn't have to work in Filler's brothel anymore. He wanted her to relax and enjoy life. She deserved a chance to live like a normal woman.

He imagined Carson tagging along and pulling at the tail of his shirt. As much as he hated playing cards with Carson, he couldn't wait to sit across from the boy and lose hand after hand to him. He missed the little face always looking at him, admiring his every move. The gleam in his eyes when James told him stories of the great Wyatt Earp. The excitement in his posture when James dreamed aloud of going on adventures and bringing Carson along. Every bit, of those moments, was more precious to James now.

James drifted off to sleep. It felt like minutes went by as his mind dreamed of getting back to town. But it turned out to be merely seconds.

James awoke the next morning to the smell of meat cooking on the fire. He opened his eyes to find Soaring Eagle roasting a prairie dog on a spit. George was still asleep, his body taking advantage of every minute of rest to recuperate.

Soaring Eagle had made breakfast for the men. They ate mostly in silence as they were all tired from the long days and nights. James fed George a broth and joked he could be George's mommy now. George just glowered at James.

Soaring Eagle packed some basic supplies for the men, including some dried meats and fruits. He stuffed some herbal tinctures and moist poultices into James' saddle bag for the trip home. He helped James load George onto his horse. James was amazed at how strong the old man was. He looked to be over seventy years old yet James felt his strength outweighed James' own.

James thanked the old man for all his help and for taking care of George. Soaring Eagle graciously accepted the thanks and told them it was all his pleasure. He wished them well and they said goodbye.

As they rode slowly along the plains, James kept turning to wave to Soaring Eagle. The little old man never moved from his spot, keeping a vigilant eye on the riders. James saw him standing there until he was so far away, he could no longer make out his figure.

CHAPTER 49

James." Carson called out to James as the men arrived in town. Carson sprung off the saloon porch and sprinted to the middle of the street. Filler heard Carson's cry and passed through the swinging doors to see for himself. James' mother also heard the cry and leaned out the bedroom window upstairs. She saw James and disappeared inside to run down the stairs to meet her son.

A small crowd gathered as they heard the commotion. Word quickly spread through town and minutes later everybody had dropped what they were doing to greet the two men. So many shouts and questions overwhelmed the men. George was still too weak to talk. Several large men helped George off his horse and carried him to Doc's room for continued treatment. James slid off his horse. Before he hit the ground Carson was wrapped around his waist, squeezing the life out of him.

"Hey buddy. How are you doing?"

"Don't ever leave me. You can't ever leave me again." Carson squeezed and begged James.

"I won't, buddy. I won't." He hugged Carson back and then ruffled his sandy hair. Carson appeared taller to James. He knew he couldn't have grown that much in a few days. But the absence had altered James' perception.

"James." Sarah pushed through the crowd and grabbed her son. She held his face in her hands. Her teary eyes searched his face, checking every inch for injuries. She squeezed him to her bosom and then backed away enough to look at his bandaged arm and bloody shirt. She looked him over and then pulled him tight again. Carson was still wrapped around James' waist so he got crushed in between James and his mother. None of them minded the intrusion of each other.

Sheriff Danvers wiggled through and clapped James on his good shoulder. He asked James for details and James only responded that it was done. The sheriff nodded, accepting the brevity of the answer for the moment. The crowd closed in and patted James on his burning back. Nobody realized he was wounded there since Soaring Eagle had wrapped his torso with bandages. The crowd cheered and some men threw their hats in the air. A sense of relief and justice rippled through the mob and, eventually, folks wandered back to their daily chores and work.

James was glad to be home.

James unpacked his horse and then worked on George's. Carson followed closely behind as James carried supplies from the saddle to the porch boards. Several times he got so close James bumped Carson's face with his rump when he backed up. James used to find it mildly annoying but loved the extra attention now. He would never take his life for granted again.

Sarah sat on the porch, witnessing the loving relationship admiringly. James smiled at his mother and she returned it, tears still filling her crystal blue eyes. James noticed for the first time just how beautiful his mother was. A few strands of her black hair fell loose from the hair clasp and swept across her face in the breeze. How could such a beautiful woman have to live such a life? He felt her start to question his staring so he busied himself with removing the rest of the supplies.

"My mom sent me a letter, you know." Carson squinted up at James. James stopped in his tracks and looked at Carson. He then looked at his mother, who smiled slightly at him.

"Oh yeah? And what did she say?"

"She said that she is doing good taking care of her relative and that she can't wait to camed home to me."

"Come. Come home to you. That's great." James glanced at his mother whose smile widened at his response and his playing along.

"And she said I can live with you and your mom until she gets back. So that makes us real brothers now." Carson acted all proud of himself for working his way into James' family officially.

James squatted down to eye level with Carson. He rested the saddle bag on the ground and placed his hands on Carson's shoulders. "You were always my brother, Carson. And you always will be." Carson hugged James, this time squeezing his neck so hard he thought his eyes would pop out of their sockets. Sarah giggled when she saw James' face wince. James pried Carson off his neck.

"Why don't you help me get this stuff upstairs? Then I'm going to take a bath and get cleaned up. And then you can come with me to visit George."

"I don't wanna visit George. He doesn't like me." Carson wrinkled his nose and folded his arms over his chest.

"George likes you, Carson. He's just funny about hiding his feelings. You know, when we went away, he told me how much he likes you and how he wished that you would hug him sometimes." Sarah gasped knowing full well that George would not like any human contact, especially from a child.

"Really?"

"Really. As a matter of fact, he said he was jealous that you always followed me around so closely. He wished you would follow him around sometimes when he is in the saloon." James winked at Carson and ruffled his hair again.

Carson seemed pleased with the notion of gaining another friend. He had only had James since he was born. His excitement of having two guys to look up to shone through his pores. The boy started to dance awkwardly, arms and legs flailing. Sarah laughed hard and tried to cover her mouth with her hand. James laughed too and stomped a foot and clapped his hands to a beat which could never synchronize with the helter skelter dance moves. James smiled at his mother.

He wanted to make things different now. He wanted to stand up and take responsibility for his mother and his little friend. No longer would he just sweep up the floors and wipe down the tables. He would get a real job for real money so the three of them could buy a place and settle down. A place they could call their home with a garden and some animals and a fence to map out their land. They would be able to eat meals together as a family instead of shoving food down, hidden in the shadows of the back of the saloon. It was time to start a new life. James was a man now. And he intended to live like one.

CHAPTER 50

I t was a little after noon but James wanted breakfast. He craved eggs and bacon, which he hadn't had in what felt like forever. Filler had the food cooked up and served "this one time on account of him being a hero and all." James took it.

He had bathed in the cool soapy water. It felt like heaven to get all the caked-on blood and dirt off his body. The soap stung his injuries though, and he found himself wincing and sucking air past his teeth each time it hurt. Carson sat on the other side of the door to keep anyone from barging in to interrupt James' bath. He knew the real reason Carson sat against the door was to ensure that his best friend couldn't leave town again without him.

James scarfed down the scrambled eggs and bacon without really chewing. The flavors were incredible compared to the earthy tastes of Soaring Eagle's cooking. Carson sat with his head in his hands watching each mouthful go in. Sarah sat across from the boys and watched too. James thought to himself both of them struggled taking their eyes off him now. It was as if they wanted to make sure he stayed within sight. Or maybe they wanted to make sure James didn't collect anymore bumps and bruises.

He swallowed the last mouthful and then burped. His mother grimaced. Carson laughed. James knew Carson loved all things pertaining to gas. It didn't matter which end it came from. James excused himself and then sat back in his chair. His stomach was full. He felt clean. And he was glad to be home.

"Feel better, honey?"

"Yes. Thanks, Mom." James got serious and then leaned over the table. "I want to take care of you. And Carson."

"You do, James."

"No, I mean really take care of you both." He looked around to make sure Filler and anybody else who might be in the saloon was outside of earshot. "I want to get a job and make money so you don't have to work here anymore. I want to get a place of our own where we can sleep and eat and raise livestock and grow crops. Not like this life here."

Sarah was taken aback by the concept. Her blue eyes searched the table to find the right words. "I don't know, James. That is an awful lot of work and requires a lot of money. We just can't afford to do that right now. I'm sorry."

"We can't do it now because I don't make anything cleaning Filler's place. But, if I got a real job, I could make some money and we could find a place and then get away from all this."

Sarah smiled at her son. "We can work on it. But it will take some time."

James sighed and folded his hands. He looked at Carson, who wasn't really following along. James began to speak but paused when Filler burst in from the back of the bar. He came in and slammed down a large crate of whiskey bottles. Feeling the eyes on him, he looked at the table. "What?"

"Nothing, Mr. Filler."

"Nothing, Mr. Filler." Filler parroted back James' response with a sarcastic tone. His pinched nose and beady eyes came together as he returned to the back room. James smiled to himself that it was indeed good to be back home, even with cranky Filler.

"I want to have a better life. We should have our own home. And enjoy ourselves as a family. Not live upstairs in a brothel. Three people in a little room. Eating on the porch like dogs." James couldn't mask his frustration. "I want to be like normal folks."

Sarah listened to her son. She could see he was serious. "You have changed, James. It's like you're all grown up now." Sarah's words didn't match the sound of doubt in voice. Her eyes reddened and welled up again.

"Aw, Mom. I've always been grown up. Nobody could see it because I was always hidden in the back."

Sarah nodded in agreement. James saw his mother was warming to the idea of him being a man and taking responsibility for their family. "Okay. We'll do it. We have to start to save though. It won't happen right away. But, if we work hard and save our money, we can do it."

James bounded out of his chair and circled the table to hug his mother. "Thanks, Mom. I'll make it work. You'll see." He held her tight. Carson, not wanting to be left out, joined in the hug. Group hugs were becoming commonplace between the three of them.

"I'm gonna get a job, too. I wanna take care of this family and buyed a house." Sarah and James laughed at how cute Carson was.

"Buy a house, Carson. And, when we get a house, there will be lots of work for you to do."

"Really? Oh boy."

James smiled. "Yeah, like cleaning the poop in the horse stables and wiping down the poop in the chicken coop and shoveling the poop in the pigpen." Carson's face wrinkled when he thought about all that poop.

"Maybe I will just help you do your work instead." He tilted his head to the side, using it to plead his case.

Sarah and James laughed out loud. Carson didn't get it but he started laughing too and then went back to dancing his awkward moves. They watched him circle the table in a happy dance. Filler burst out of the back room again. His face screwed up the second he saw the family carrying on at the table. He slammed another crate of booze down on the bar.

"Hey. I ain't paying ya to whoop it up and have a good time, ya know," his anger coming through loud and clear.

"No, you don't pay us at all. Do you?" James sassed Filler back. The man wrung his beard and then put his hands on his hips in frustration. The family saw his reaction and the three of them burst into laughter. Filler stomped his feet and cursed obscenities not known to regular mankind. But that didn't stop Sarah, James and Carson from laughing. In fact, Sarah and James jumped out of their seats and joined Carson in the dance around the table.

CHAPTER 51

The evening sky had a purplish hue. James sat on the back porch with Carson. They had finished their dinner and now Carson was shuffling the deck of cards. He had talked about playing the whole time they ate. James enjoyed the excitement that poured through Carson's words, as he rambled on about how he had nobody to play with over the last few days. But he had practiced his shuffling skills and now he could do it much faster.

James tuned Carson out as he reflected on his life. Since he could remember, he had dreamed about growing up to follow in his father's legendary footsteps. Moving from town to town. Tangling with drunks and cheats. Chasing off cattle rustlers. Gunfights in the street. In his eyes, life could only be lived on a grand scale as a hero. As the center of attention.

His thoughts were different now. Life was more about living each moment because you never knew when a curse would take everything away from you. It was being with the people you loved and cared for, because they could die tomorrow and you would no longer see their face or hear their voice. Life was a responsibility to yourself and your family, making sure that people were loved and fed and protected. Not hanging around looking for something to do to pass the time until the next meal. Not dreaming about someday which may or may not ever arrive.

James glanced at Carson who was oblivious, shuffling and re-shuffling the deck of cards while talking a mile a minute. Life was work. It wasn't meant to be easy. Everyone had their cross to bear. Carson fought every day to be considered normal, one of the townspeople, a member of the family. His life was hard. Always made fun of or ignored. James' mother toiled with dirty men every night to feed her son. She had to work hard to maintain her appearance so she was desirable enough to earn customers who then disrespected her. And the townspeople didn't really respect her either. Girls like her were referred to as whores and sluts in hushed conversations or the pews of the church.

Even men like Sheriff Danvers and Wilson and George had their crosses. Working hard to instill the law in a land full of wild people. Struggling with being a drunk and not being able to hold a job or function like a regular person. Living to fight with your bare hands day in and day out. The physical abuse of a fighting lifestyle, breaking down joints and bones over time.

James thought about Crouching Bear, his lost friend. He bore the cross of his tribe's warring ways. He was cast out because of a mistake made in the fever of battle, which should never have happened, if his elders had done the right thing by their tribe and lived peacefully to protect their own. Instead, he was cursed and forced to live a solitary existence, running from the next battle, only to end up dead by his friend's hand.

He turned his thoughts to his own life. Growing up without a father. With a whore for a mother. Living like an unwanted pet in the back of a saloon. Never being taken seriously because he was the illegitimate son of a whore. Owning the responsibility of getting his friend's mother killed, of killing another one of his friends, and taking care of a slow boy.

Life was work. It was difficult. But it was still worth living. It wasn't the larger moments, the years of living here or working there. Life was about the small moments. Tunneling out a hiding spot with someone special. Giving your mother a flower on her birthday. Helping an outcast find comfort when they have nowhere else to turn. Those were the moments that made life real.

James pondered the idea of no longer wanting big adventures. The notion of living quietly on the outskirts of town. Watching his mother plant seeds. Seeing Carson run wild in the fields. That would be enough.

As soon as he imagined this peaceful life, something stirred in his gut. He sat up straight. Deep inside, a struggle took place, a strong calling that would not sit idle. He felt the temptation of adventure rumbling in his belly, a restlessness that could not be satisfied with a quiet town life. James squirmed and tried to push away the feeling. But it would not be cast aside.

Carson tapped his shoulder and asked him if he was ready to play cards now. James smiled down at Carson and nodded. His mind still far away, fighting evil. There were evil beings harming others. Everywhere. He knew it was the truth but he questioned what it had to do with him. He wasn't a hero. He wasn't a mythic character put on earth to battle the forces of evil. He was just a man, a man who wanted to be with his family.

But he knew the real truth. James couldn't accept this life. He couldn't sit still knowing that people needed help. James saw the faces of people crying in sorrow, screaming in horror and hiding in fear. He knew those faces even if he didn't know the actual people they belonged to.

His life had changed. In growing up, he had not only become a man. He had also become a spirit of something bigger. A warrior like his lost friend. He smiled when he thought of Crouching Bear with him and Carson at their hiding spot.

James looked at the hand of cards he was dealt. He had a four of clubs, a seven of hearts, an ace of spades, and a pair of fives. The lousy hand made him chuckle to himself. He watched Carson fan out his cards, his eyes darting back and forth as he organized the hand. James put his cards down, faces up. He looked at Carson, who was perplexed with James' early folding. Then he spoke in a serious tone but with a grin on his face.

"What do you think about going on an adventure with me?"

DIRECTOR'S CUT

This story was a ton of fun to write.

Like many young boys, I grew up desperate for my father's approval. Forty-odd years later, nothing has changed. I still desperately seek his approval on just about everything. So one day, I casually mentioned I wanted to be a horror writer. The reception was pretty much what I would have expected. He gave me a look like he had just bitten into a rotten tomato.

My father has always been a voracious reader, easily devouring a book a week since I can first remember. But horror is not on ANY of his reading lists. A child of the 50s, my father was (and still is) a huge fan of westerns and country music. My father worshiped John Wayne and Louis L'Amour. Somewhere in his mind, he's probably the man who shot Liberty Valance.

So what better way to earn my father's praise than to write a western novel? I know. Writing a western horror novel. Two birds, one stone. Once I decided to embark on this journey, the character of James Johnson (nee Earp) formed immediately. Everyone loves the legendary men of the old west. But what about the people that might have been left behind?

It made sense to me that a man like Wyatt Earp could have fathered a child out of wedlock with a prostitute. Who hasn't? Ahem. I mean, it could have happened to anyone. But who would care if it happened to some random cowpoke?

Like many good westerns, the hero usually has a sidekick. These sidekicks provide comic relief or further support the hero's journey. I wanted to use the sidekick to accomplish similar goals but through the optics of a new twist. My original concept was for a female sidekick but I was afraid somewhere down the line, the story would call for the relationship to take on a more romantic tone. I am not opposed to a formidable male/female duo but it didn't strike me as original enough. That's where Carson came in.

Several members of my family were involved in special education careers. For years, I heard stories about children who struggled with basic functions, things we take for granted. I also know families with autistic children. Carson is somewhere in between, but completely different. He holds an intelligence level that can be remarkable. Yet, he struggles as a functioning member of society. It is natural to feel sorry for him and root for him like crazy.

I hope you enjoyed reading this story as much as I did writing it. I really like James and Carson as people, not just characters in a book. So I think you can expect to hear more from them in the future.

Chuck Buda

P.S. I hope you will join us in Book 2 to find out what rolls into town with the tumbleweeds.

I feel safer with you by my side.

ABOUT THE AUTHOR

Chuck Buda explores the darkest aspects of the human condition. Then he captures its essence for fictional use. He writes during the day and wanders aimlessly all night…alone.

Chuck Buda co-hosts The Mando Method Podcast on Project Entertainment Network with author, Armand Rosamilia. They talk about all aspects of writing. Subscribe so you don't miss an episode. You can find The Mando Method Podcast on iTunes, Stitcher and most other places where podcasts are available. Or you can listen directly from the Project Entertainment Network website.

www.PROJECTENTERTAINMENTNETWORK.com